Best wishes John.

Lee

# Pickit

## By

## Lee Richardson

London, August 1816. "The year without a summer."

London is heaving with a society, which ranged from the rich, living in their fine houses, their mansions and palaces, and the poor, living in hovels and squalor.

Pickit is eighteen years old. He was abandoned at birth, and unlucky enough to be found by a woman, who lived off the criminal activities of those in her care. The lad only escaped her clutches after her untimely demise.

Fending for himself, he managed to gain some financial security and lodgings, by caretaking a warehouse. The warehouse housed illicit goods, as the owner was a successful smuggler, but that did not faze Pickit at all. The smuggler paid well.

Colonel James Robert Tyler was born in 1790. His Mother died when he was just a boy of thirteen, and his father, remarried a little time later. James had to leave and make his own way in life, due to a series of arguments with his stepmother. He was fifteen years of age.

In 1806, when he was just sixteen, James joined the army and made the rank of Colonel in 1813. After serving under Sir Arthur Wellesley and surviving the Battle of Waterloo, he returned to London. His best friend died in the battle, and left him his entire estate, making James a wealthy man.

Pickit and James's paths should never have crossed, but fate had other ideas.

*Chapter 1*


The passage was dark, dank and filthy. It stank of raw sewage and rotting food. Straw, animal corpses and other unrecognisable filth were trapped in gratings and piled in doorways. Each passage and alley was an entryway to another even narrower thoroughfare. The area was a mass of crumbling, badly built and poorly lit hovels, heaving with the dregs of society.

Oftentimes, ten, fifteen and even twenty people crammed themselves into one small room, throwing their waste into the gutters, running the centre of each street or alley. The gullies emptied straight into the Thames. The better tenements relied on night-soil men and hand pumped water.

The lad did not notice the slime clinging to his bare feet and legs. The foul air invaded his lungs, but he was familiar with it, and did not care. He was too busy running full pelt, the sound of heavy boots and shouts of "Stop him!" and "Thief!" ringing in his ears.

He ducked into a narrow passage, dodging men, women, children and dogs. The passage was heaving with people of every description. Each alley, filthier than the first, led deeper into the maze of St Giles, a territory this lad knew very well.

A man scruffily dressed and reeking of cheap gin stumbled his way along the alley and collided with Pickit. The man fell to the ground, and obviously beyond caring, just lay where he had fallen. People stared out of grimy, cracked windows patched with filthy rags and greased paper. Their blank stares were a sign of their hopeless plight.

The sound of heavy footfalls and the shouting was becoming fainter with every step he trod. Within minutes, he could hear nothing but the slapping of his own bare flesh on stone, and the hacking cough of an old hag dressed in an assortment of rags, lying in a doorway. His pursuers had run out of steam, or had more than likely lost all sense of direction in the intricate weave of narrow alleyways, that crisscrossed 1816 London.

No decent person would want to enter this place alone. Occasionally, a man uneducated in the ways of the criminal underworld, would enter this foul, rancid place in pursuit of some ragtag who had lifted his purse. The man, would in all probability, never be seen again. If found, he would have been stripped of his finery, money and jewellery and beaten half to death or murdered, and left to rot where he lay. Other people might step over him, or drag him into a gully or drain for his remains to be swept away at the rising of the tide.

The boy stopped, and leant with his back against a wall which was wet with rivulets of grey, stinking water, that seeped from somewhere above his head. A rat, the size of a small dog, scuttled across the alley and through a hole in the wall. Gasping to suck the fetid air into his lungs, he bent and placed his filthy hands on his knees, and the pulse throbbing in his ears was almost deafening. Snot dripped from his nose, which he wiped away with a torn, ragged shirtsleeve, then wiped his hot, sweaty face. The thought of the wallet and gold watch packed tightly inside the shirt, which barely covered his filthy, emaciated body, comforted him. He would eat well tonight, the first time in many days. The theft had gone badly though, the victim, keenly aware of pickpockets and cutpurses, had reached out and tried to grab the lad. Pickit ducked under the man's out-stretched arm, and ran swiftly away with the clamour of "Stop thief!" ringing in his ears.

When his heavy breathing and the 'stitch' digging at his side had eased, he made his way along the dark alley, too narrow for a carriage, and with barely enough room to walk two abreast. He made his way down towards the Strand and the river. The tide would be up and he could wash some of the foulness away, without having to tread in the stinking mud.

The Thames did not yield the cleanest of water; he would be the first to admit. However, he had to remove some of the grime and sewage embedded in his sallow skin. Even the most unscrupulous of the street vendors would not serve him in his present state, worried that the lad's filthy appearance might draw the keen eye of a Thief-Taker or Bow Street Runner.

Pickit, not his real name of course, for he did not know his real name, was named for his skills. He was a Mug Hunter and Tooler of the highest order, for if something could be picked, whether it was a lock, a pocket, or a safe, he could pick it. Picking pockets and locks were not his only skills. He had many more awaiting an opportune moment.

Pickit was just eighteen years of age, though if told his age, he would have shrugged his bony shoulders with a 'couldn't-care-less' attitude, which he often adopted when faced with a problem he could not solve. He may have been only eighteen, but he had lived a few lifetimes in the sewers, the alleyways and the mudflats of the stinking waters of the Thames. These areas were where he often scrounged for anything that would bring in a penny.

His mother, a woman of somewhat ill repute, had given birth to him on the steps of a local hostelry by the name of The Grapes of Wrath. It had burned down under suspicious circumstances a short time afterwards.

Upon taking his first breath, he had been left to fight his own corner. Fortunately, or perhaps unfortunately, a woman of undetermined years, and dubious reputation found him just in time, before his little body had turned completely blue from the cold night air. She took him in, reared him on meagre rations and taught him, along with a few others, the ways of the world. This included pick pocketing, breaking and entering, general thievery, robbery with violence, and anything else her criminal mind could imagine Pickit had not yet murdered anyone, but he had the expertise and would be able to dispatch anyone, should the need arise.

One night, during a bitter cold spell with winds that could blow down trees and sink ships, 'Mother' as everyone knew her, went out to replenish her stock of gin, paid for by the ill-gotten gains of the waifs and strays she called 'her babies'. She was never seen again.

Pickit was twelve years old then, and although not the eldest, he was certainly the brightest. He had arranged for the five younger children, all under the age of eight, to be collected and taken to the nearest home for orphans, paupers and the destitute, run by the local church. He gave the money, which he had found under the floorboards of the hovel they called home, to the church by way of a donation. He knew that the children would not benefit and in all probability would end up in a workhouse or may not survive to their adult years. The two older children, a girl of sixteen or so, and a boy aged about fourteen sporting a mop of bright red hair, were told to make their own way in life, as he had to do himself. The two, argued that they should stay together.

Pickit knew from experience that he would be the one doing all the work, whilst the girl and the boy enjoyed the spoils. Pickit scoffed loudly at the idea of all of them staying on in this putrid hovel and, although the argument was heated and threatening, he stood his ground. He told them that they could stay together for all he cared, but he was going to lead his own life.

For six years, he had managed to stay one-step ahead of serious trouble, though he did spend a short time in Newgate for attacking a sailor who had tried to take advantage of him. He did not mix with the others down on the mudflats, unless it was necessary, believing that the only person he could trust was himself. That belief had stood him in good stead over the years, and when others had been killed, injured or jailed, he stood apart on the fringes looking on, knowing that he had to rely on his own survival instincts or end up like them.

Pickit stood and watched silently as the freezing cold water lapped at his feet, caressing, cleaning, and cooling. Though the smell of the river was pungent, at low tide the stench, which assailed the nostrils, was so overpowering it could make eyes water and stomachs churn.

Chapter 2

It was beginning to get dark, but the full moon had not yet crept up over the rooftops. He had washed his shirt in the muddy, stinking waters and had wrung it out as well as he could. It was now hanging precariously from a twig, which was attached to a leafless bush, which only survived by sheer will power, in the mud and slime. The wind had risen and the ragged shirt flapped in the breeze. He hoped it would be dry before full darkness.

He bent and scooped up the water, throwing it over his face and head. It trickled down his naked torso, making his teeth chatter. Immediately, he felt re-vitalised, ready for action, ready for anything.

The lad knew from experience, that he would have to be alert here. Some, commonly known as 'Mudlarks', were also dabbling in the cold waters. Some were washing clothes; others were foraging for anything that could be utilised for example, bottles, metal, coal and anything else that might make a penny or two. A few others loitered, furtively watching, faces obscured by tattered scarves or collars. These were not merely thieves but violent thugs of the most dangerous kind, the kind, who would kill if the mood took them. They would target anyone they thought might be carrying money or re-saleable goods, including young children.

Watching the 'mudlarks' rake through the mud and silt of the river, they would pounce if something of value was found. Pickit had learnt the hard way; he never scavenged in the mud. Some of the lads here were friends, but he would not have trusted them as far as he could spit into the wind. The wallet stolen earlier had been emptied and discarded. He had dumped it on a rat infested rubbish mound, and the money it had contained was now tucked away as safely as it could be. The watch, not required by a lad who had no concept of time, had been hawked and the spoils added to the money from the wallet.

One of the major advantages of Pickit's miserable life was his ability to count. He had watched as 'mother' had counted out the money, which had been brought to her by her 'charges'. He had quickly learned from her mumblings, the value of each coin and note. Now, somewhere in the network of passages and alleys, near to the place he called home, there was a hole in the wall, where he kept a stash of money, hidden by a loose brick. The boy had carefully camouflaged that part of the wall. It was so murky in that alley that you would be lucky to find your way with half a dozen flaming torches after dark, and the filthy footings ensured that you never took your eyes off the steps, which you trod, during daylight. This was Pickit's stepping-stone out of the deprivation and misery, which he suffered on a daily basis.

He wiped his hands on his breeches and threw the slightly damp shirt over his head. Darkness was falling all too quickly now, and he moved away from the river and up on to the street. The damp shirt next to his skin made him shiver and he wished he had a coat.

He sensed, rather than saw, the figure moving towards him and Pickit quickened his step, wanting to reach one of the feeble gas-lit thoroughfares. People were making their way home from the theatre, or moving to or from the gin-palaces, dram-shops and taverns, or just strolling, enjoying the summer evening. He could hear the footsteps getting closer. Though the only money he had on him was, the two pennies needed to pay for his supper. He was in no mood to take the beating that would accompany any theft, from his person, so as soon as his bare feet touched the cobbles, he was away, as swift as a gazelle with the wind behind her.

A few minutes later, the boy slowed to a fast walk as he mingled with carriages and other people on the street. He glanced back, but could not see his pursuer. Pickit paced himself, but could not relax, knowing he might still be jumped upon, though that was getting less likely by the minute. Whoever had been on his tail would not risk a stampede for just a couple of pennies.

He caught sight of a pie-man on the corner of The Strand and Drury Lane, and made his way towards the street vendor. It was not easy avoiding other pedestrians, horses, carriages, and butcher's stalls, whilst glancing over his shoulder every few steps. He made himself relax, knowing his stalker would be long gone, looking for easier prey, and no doubt realising that Pickit was far too perceptive to be taken off guard.

After paying for and taking the hot pie, Pickit made his way through the crowd to a low wall, which fronted a rather dubious establishment with two scantily clad women chattering at the door. One nodded in his direction, "Want a good time me beauty?" Pickit glared at her. "Bin a long time since I cuddled such an 'andsome lad", she cackled, showing her toothless gums. "Half price to you me 'andsome." He ignored her and sat down, watching the street for a moment. From here, he could not see the river, as warehouses and rambling tenements lined the waterfront, but he could smell it. The stench of it was everywhere.

The evening was quite cool; in fact, there had not been what you would call a summer, as most days had been overcast, dull and quite cold. Despite the chill in the air, the street was busy. Carriages rumbled along the thoroughfare, carrying their passengers to their homes, or to some form of entertainment. The clatter of horses' hooves', people shouting and a few street musicians added to the melee. A boy of about seven, as thin as a pole, dressed in his red jacket, was gathering the horse droppings and shovelling them into a small wooden wheelbarrow. That little waif would earn enough to get his supper tonight.

Pickit sat watching the crowd, some people busy in conversation with a companion, or a group of men laughing at a joke, or earnestly discussing something of importance. Some were plying their trade, calling out to the crowd. Food could be bought, shoes could be cobbled or cleaned, and clothes, hardware, or household furniture could be purchased. Anything you required could be bought for a price in this locality, including a companion for the night, either male or female. The storekeepers and barrow traders would be here selling their goods until late into the night. They would be back by eight a.m. on the morrow.

Finishing the last of his pie, Pickit stood and licked his fingers. He heard the sounds of a disturbance. People started moving aside, and one young dandy collided with a carriage rumbling down the street. He had missed the horse's hooves and the wheels of the coach by inches, as he landed on the filthy cobbles, but only his pride was hurt. Pickit leapt up onto the wall where he had been sitting only a few moments before, and stared in the direction of the melee. The crowd was making way for a man who was running for his life. He was still some distance away and the boy could not see who was chasing him. As the quarry approached the place where Pickit was standing, the boy could see him beginning to falter. The man stumbled then gained his footing, but the mistake had cost him dearly, for his pursuers had gained a few steps and were now hot on his heels. Pickit counted pursuers, settling on a figure of five or six. The quarry would be run down very soon.

As the man approached, Pickit leapt from the wall, and running alongside to set the pace, grabbed the man's sleeve yelling, "Follow me!"

For a moment, the man looked startled, and then gained his composure. They ran on into a dark, narrow street, which the man recognised as Newcastle Street, which led to Drury Lane. The street, illuminated only by the dim light emitted from the few shops. The tavern tucked away off the thoroughfare, was as busy as anywhere on this night. The pair had to avoid stragglers rather the worse for drink, wandering about aimlessly. They ran on, knocking into those not quick enough to get out of their way. One man, short of leg and rather portly, tried to stop them, but found himself on his backside in an open sewer. His friends doubled up with laughter at the sight of their acquaintance wallowing in the mud. The pair turned on to Drury Lane, then on to Russel Street heading for Covent Garden.

Pickit glanced back over his shoulder; he could see that the baying crowd had been left far behind on the thoroughfare. One minute, the lad and the stranger were in sight, no more than fifteen feet away and close enough to touch. It seemed as though they had vanished right before their eyes. Now they were trying to decide in which direction, the pair had gone.

Pickit led his new charge towards an alley that would lead them to safety. They ran on until their footsteps were the only sounds that they could hear. As they approached Bow Street, Pickit put out his hand to indicate that they should stop. They had reached the junction of Hart Street. The boy looked up and down the cobbled alley; a few people lingered in doorways, or sat on grimy doorsteps, but no one paid them any attention. "We have to take care here; the 'robin redbreasts' hang around in these parts," Pickit said, softly.

"Robin who?" the man gasped.

"Bow Street Runners," Pickit explained, eyes darting in all directions.

"Come on, not far now," Pickit urged, as the man bent over holding his side.

He thought his lungs were on fire and would burst at any moment. He was gasping for air, his legs were trembling and he thought he might be sick. He leant against the filthy wall trying to dispel his nausea.

"Not much further now," Pickit grinned.

The man shook his head. "No, wait please, I'm dying."

"You'll be fine, come on, we can't hang about around here; the Runners will be after us. We're on their doorstep, come on, move!" He grabbed the man's arm, half pulled, and half shoved the stranger across the street and into a narrow passageway.

"Where are we, what is this place?" the man gasped, promising himself that he would try to keep fit in future, and would walk everywhere instead of taking a carriage. He never used to feel so ill after running short distances; he had fought a war for goodness sake.

"We'll be on St Martin's in a tick," Pickit explained.

"Thank goodness," the man said, sardonically. He looked around at the squalor.

"Well, we know our way all around here, we do, and we can double back and actually taunt those after us, confuses 'em no end it do," Pickit said.

"I bet it do, er does, and who is 'we'?" the man asked, his chest still heaving. A cutting pain dug deeply in his left side.

Pickit shrugged his shoulders but said nothing. He led the stranger along the alley apparently fronted by warehouses. He walked quickly, the man having some difficulty keeping up with the boy.

"I can get home from here," the man said.

"Wouldn't advise it," Pickit said.

"Why?"

Pickit stopped and pointed at his dirty fingers as if counting. "It's dark now and there be footpads, thieves, pickpockets, thugs, murder…"

The man held up his hands in surrender. "Alright, alright, but just tell me, where are you taking me?"

Pickit grinned. "You can't wander around here by yourself, that's for sure. I am taking you to my place. Then, as soon as it's light, I can lead you out of here and put you on the right road."

The stranger felt trapped, and the boy caught the look of doubt that crossed his face.

"I won't rob you and I won't hurt you. Honest," Pickit said, holding a hand against his heart.

The man smiled, "Well, I don't suppose I have much choice. If I don't die at your hands, it would be at another's hands.

Pickit shook his head, "Just trust me, I ain't as bad as I look."

The boy led the way up Newport Street and through more narrow passages, up and on to Church Street. The whole area reeked of poverty and deprivation. The man did not think things could get worse, but they did. The streets were narrow, barely wider than a passage, the eves of the houses almost touching across the street. Filth was strewn all around and foul water ran down walls and into the narrow trenches hewn out of the uneven cobbles. Turning a corner, they arrived at a wooden fronted building.

It looked nothing like a house, a warehouse nor workshop. There were no windows on the ground floor, just double fronted doors, tightly chained and padlocked. A rickety, wooden staircase, tucked away at the side between this and the adjacent building, led to the upper floors. The stranger followed the boy as he led him up three flights of stairs until they arrived at a wooden door set into the wall. The door could not be seen from the ground. Pickit, looking all around for signs of life, fiddled with a loose stone over the doorjamb and brought out a candle and a tinderbox. Producing a rusting iron key, he unlocked the rather solid door, which swung back with barely a creak of its well-oiled hinges. He lit the candle and entered the gloomy hovel; the stranger, mouth agape, stared at the dingy, twelve by twelve feet square room with its soot covered walls and damp floorboards. "You live here?" he asked, incredulously.

Pickit nodded, and dragged a wooden crate up to a rickety, homemade table, consisting of a few planks of wood across the top of a brown, stained, tea chest. He stuck the candle in a candleholder on the otherwise bare tabletop.

Another smaller box served as a makeshift seat, and the only other pieces of furniture in the room were a pallet containing a filthy straw mattress and a couple of moth eaten, coarse, woollen blankets. A sea chest stood at the side of the pallet bed. A skylight in the roof would have been the only source of light during the day, but now a cluster of stars was all that could be seen through the grimy glass. One wall contained a filthy grate, inches deep in ash, with a chimney over it. A small iron chest stood at the side of the fireplace. The stranger sat on the proffered seat and gawped at his surroundings.

"The owner pays me a few pennies a week to look after the place. Well, when he remembers, that is. Stores things here he does. Big crates and boxes he gets off the ships. I am not supposed to say anything to anyone. This place, 'tis better than some you could find yourself in. A palace compared to some. Cold in here it is though," Pickit announced, fiddling with his dirty shirt.

"It is cold. I have spent too much time in warmer climes to get used to this in a hurry," the stranger said.

Pickit grinned. "I'd better make a fire then."

"You don't have to make a fire on my account."

"I have to make one. It gets too cold up here; I'd freeze to death in my sleep."

He suddenly felt embarrassed at his clothing, for in the candlelight, he could now see that the stranger was dressed in the fashionable and probably expensive clothes of the day. He wore a tall hat, gold coloured waistcoat, a deep blue, double-breasted, high-collared frockcoat and cream coloured, tight pantaloons tucked into leather, knee length boots. The cravat at his throat was tied in the latest fashion and was brilliant white. The stranger removed his hat, showing a full head of dark collar length hair with fashionable side-whiskers, framing a handsome face. Pickit presumed he was in his mid to late twenties.

The boy had busied himself with the fireplace, and had now removed the ash to a metal bucket from which he had removed some kindling, a piece of rag and a few lumps of coal. Within minutes, he had lit a fire in the grate. He had hung a kettle-pot of water, on a hook over the fire.

The stranger examined his surroundings. "I'm known as James Tyler, and what is your name?"

"People call me Pickit," the boy replied.

"Where is your family?" The man coughed and wafted the smoke away.

Pickit shrugged his shoulders. "No family, just me," he explained. "I was found on the street as a baby, never knew my mam or dad, or if I ever even had one, just some old crone who took me in and reared me."

*Chapter 3*

James Robert Tyler had enlisted in the army at the age of sixteen. His father had remarried, having lost his first wife, James's mother, when the boy was thirteen. Two years later his father had remarried. James and his stepmother did not see eye-to-eye, and as time went on, he became more and more rebellious, until he would no longer comply with anything asked of him. On James fifteenth birthday, his father a successful merchant, gave James a purse of coins and told him to seek his fortune out in the world.

James enlisted at the rank of Cornet in the Cavalry. He first saw action when French armies led by Napoleon, invaded Portugal in 1807. In 1813, the Sixth Coalition defeated Napoleon's forces at Leipzig, and the following year the Coalition invaded France. Napoleon was forced to abdicate and was exiled to the island of Elba. Less than a year later, Napoleon escaped from the island and returned to power. By this time, Tyler had bought and fought his way up to the rank of Major in the Life Guards.

Tyler served at the Battle of Waterloo under Arthur Wellesley, the 1st Duke of Wellington, commander of the allied British, Dutch and German troops, and General Blücher led Prussia against the French, fighting under the command of Napoleon. Tyler, who had served successfully in the campaigns, had returned home from the Napoleonic Wars, victorious. He gained the rank of Colonel, in Napoleon's final defeat, on the battlefield of a village named Waterloo, which was eight miles south of Brussels.

He had been a competent leader and fearless fighter, who could be relied upon by those around him to stand his ground against the most aggressive of foes. He had suffered only minor injuries, including the loss of the small finger on his left hand, when an over exuberant French soldier had tried to pierce him with a lance, and the Colonel had used the hand to thwart the blow. He did not realise his loss until a fellow officer had pointed to the injured hand saying, "I believe you may have lost something Colonel."

James glanced down at the injury now dripping with blood. "Good Lord, That has put 'paid' to any ambitions I had of becoming a concert pianist," they had both laughed.

The French lancer had not fared so well and had died for his trouble.

Two days after James had lost his finger, the officer that had been beside him, lost his life. His name was Sir George Alexander Radcliffe. His ancestors had originally hailed from East Anglia. His father, Lord Radcliffe, had married a much younger woman following the death of his barren first wife. He had sold off the family estate, and moved new wife and baby George to London to keep an eye on his other successful businesses and interests.

They had met when they had enlisted together in 1806, and had become firm friends. Then on that fateful day, during the battle of Waterloo, a well-aimed cannon ball had taken off George's head. James sat there in total shock, watching as George's headless corpse, slid of the horse and landed on the ground with a thud.

The death of George spurred him on to declare that he would kill as many Frenchmen as he could. Unfortunately, for James, combined English and Prussian forces defeated Napoleon on Sunday 18th June 1815; the day after George was killed. The battle of Waterloo had lasted three days.

Tyler had nightmares for days, and intermittently, for months. In his dreams, George's head, now lying in the mud, spoke to him, pleading with him to help him. Not long after that fateful day, the Lieutenant Colonel commanding his unit, informed him that Colonel Radcliffe had left a letter for him. They had only just found it in his belongings.

*Dear James,*

*If you are reading this, I am no longer in the land of the living. I do hope I went out in a blaze of glory and not under the wheels of a coal cart, or murdered for a few pennies by a thief or a vagabond.*

*It is such dammed bad luck on my part old chap that I may have left without knowing the love and tenderness of a beautiful woman, or without spending a farthing of Papa's money. I therefore charge you to do these things for me or at least in my honour.*

*There will be a fellow named Banks awaiting your acquaintance, the details of which can be found in the enclosed document. Do give him my best regards; and I can assure you that Banks can be trusted with your life and all your worldly possessions.*

*Enjoy your new life, travel and explore, fall in love with every beautiful woman you meet, marry and have many wonderful children, Never be afraid of anything again as I shall be watching over you.*

*Sir George Alexander Radcliffe, Col.*

*Chapter 4*

Tyler knew that George had a nice little inheritance tucked away, and the unexpected windfall about to come his way, cushioned the blow somewhat for him. It was not until he had returned to England, that he realised the full extent of his benefaction.

Colonel James Robert Tyler returned to London five weeks later, and presented himself at the stately residence of the mysterious Banks, as instructed in the letter he had received from George via his Commanding Officer.

"Ah! Major Tyler, please do come into my office." Henry Banks ushered James into a large, beautifully furnished room dominated with a mahogany desk. Bookshelves covered two walls from floor to ceiling, and a large window behind the desk looked over towards St James' Park. Banks ushered James towards a plush chair and told him to make himself comfortable. He rang a small brass bell, which had been sitting on the desk. As he sat opposite Tyler, there was a knock at the door.

Banks shuffled a stack of papers into a neat pile, calling "Come in!" as he tidied the desk. "Ah there you are Fielding," he said, to a thin boy of about sixteen years. The young man was dressed all in black. His black hair, hunched back and hooked nose, gave him the appearance of a rook. "Would you please bring tea? Unless of course," he peered at his client, "you would prefer something a little stronger perhaps, Major Tyler?"

"Tea would be fine and it's Colonel Tyler by the way. Unless I have been relieved of my commission and someone has forgotten to tell me." he smiled.

Banks smiled. "Of course Colonel, please do forgive me. I had forgotten your very well deserved promotion," he turned to the boy. "And would you ask Sir Charles to join us?" The lad bowed and backed out of the room. Sir Henry leant forward; "Sir Charles Collins is not only my best friend, but also a very astute man when it comes to business," he whispered, conspiratorially. "He is here to ensure that everything is carried out according to George's wishes."

Just over an hour later, Colonel James Robert Tyler was legally a very rich man, and the owner of a house in a cul-de-sac, off St James's Street, not far from Pall Mall. He also had interests in various businesses including a plantation in the Americas and a small sheep farm in Australia. A mine on the Australian property had not been worked in years, as it had not yielding anything of value. "Why has George, er, Colonel Radcliffe, left all this to me?" James had asked during the meeting. "Surely he has other family, or close friends."

Lord Henry Banks had shaken his head. "I'm afraid not, Colonel. George's father died many years ago of Typhoid sadly. He was a dear, dear friend who made sure, that I would always be prosperous, and all because I advised him on a few lucrative investments. He sent his friends to me, business associates, even people he barely knew," Banks stood up and looked out of the window. "A good man was Lord Radcliffe, and because of him, I shall never starve and neither will my children or grandchildren. His wife Jane, George's mother, was a real lady, beautiful to look at and beautiful within. She was many years younger than her husband, of course, but she adored him. It almost killed her when he died, but she hung on for George's sake. She died in 1812 from the same illness that had killed her husband. George was their only child, but there had been a girl, but sadly, she died in infancy. It had been a difficult pregnancy and a traumatic birth.

Unfortunately, there had been no other children; a fact that saddened them both as originally, a large family had been planned. I know this may sound callous, but in a way, I am glad that Jane had died when she did. She simply could not have borne the grief of losing George at such a young age."

For a few moments, there was silence. Then Tyler cleared his throat. "Lord Banks, you have been very kind and are obviously astute and shrewd in all business matters. You have taken care of George's business for all these years, and his father's before him. Would you please continue to do so for me? I cannot comprehend the amount that George has bequeathed to me, and I really do feel unworthy."

Lord Banks, his hands behind his back, turned and looked at Tyler. "My dear Colonel, George knew what he was doing, so please receive it in the spirit it was given. I would be delighted, and nothing would give me greater pleasure than to attend to your financial matters," he beamed. "I will have Sir Charles arrange the necessary legal papers."

James grinned sheepishly then stood and turned to leave.

"There is one more thing Colonel," Banks was holding a bunch of keys. "I have left the afternoon free, as I know the property rather well and would love to show you around, but if you would prefer to explore your new home on your own, I would understand of course. It is only takes a few minutes to walk from here and the weather has improved somewhat. Ideal for a stroll, don't you think?" he was grinning.

"I think that would be a grand idea." James grabbed his hat.

A little while later, they entered a cul-de-sac just off St James's Street, "This is the property." Banks stopped in front of an imposing building.

Tyler looked at the white, four storey, and double fronted house, with its seven broad steps. It was flanked by black, ornate railings, which led up to the black door with its fan styled window above and flanked by high windows either side. Black, newly painted ornate railings, stood before the building, and at the end, a wrought iron gate opened onto five steps, which led down to the basement rooms. The second storey consisted of three high windows, each fronted by a small balcony. These were surrounded by the same type of wrought iron railings as on the first floor. The third floor consisted of three windows though only half the size of those on the second floor.

"I have kept it in good repair whilst Master George was away," Sir Henry pursed his lips. "I can't get used to the fact that he won't be returning."

"I know how you feel, Sir. For eight years, we were inseparable, he was my right arm." James rubbed his hands together. It was cold for a summer afternoon and he was feeling the chill.

Sir Henry nodded. "Master George told me a lot about you Colonel, I probably know as much about you as he did."

"Really?" James asked with surprise.

Sir Henry smiled. "Didn't you know? He held you in great esteem."

Both were quiet as Banks pulled the keys from his pocket. "Just one question, Colonel, and I'll never ask you anything again," he fiddled with the keys.

James nodded. "Ask away Sir, I'll answer any questions you care to ask, if I can."

"Did he suffer?" Sir Henry looked down at the pavement. He was head and shoulders shorter than Tyler, stocky, with slightly bandy legs sheathed in black, silk stockings. He also wore patent shoes, decorated with silver buckles, on his feet.

"I can say with my hand on my heart, that George never felt a thing. I will say one thing though," James hesitated.

"Yes?" Banks urged.

"George died a hero. He was not afraid of anything or anyone, and he faced all our enemies head on. I am proud to have known him, Sir Henry."

Banks nodded. "Me too, Colonel, me too." He knocked on the door with his cane.

"Does someone live here?" James asked.

Banks smiled. "Only the servants, well, as far as I know. I would usually let myself in, but they don't know who you are, and it would worry them if I walked in with a stranger." James nodded in his understanding.

"Of course, if there is no one at home, as sometimes happens, then I will use the keys."

"Servants? How many servants?" James asked, though before he received an answer, a man of about 45 years opened the door.

"Good afternoon, Sir Henry. Good afternoon, Colonel Tyler." The man bowed slightly, and stood aside to allow the two men inside.

"He knows my name," James whispered. Banks just smiled.

"Will you please ask the others to meet us in the drawing room, Arthur?" The man bowed ever so slightly.

23

"Of course, sir," he replied.

James stood with his mouth open. Before them, a wide sweeping staircase led to the upper floors. Banks showed James into the large, beautifully furnished room on the right. A tall window, furnished with cream brocade drapes, looked out over the mews.

A few minutes later, a slender woman, in her late forties appeared. Her greying hair was tied at the nape of her neck and she wore a white mobcap. A young girl, in her early twenties, with a striking resemblance to Arthur, followed him into the room.

"This is Mrs Ash, she is the cook and housekeeper here, and this is Lizzie, kitchen help and housemaid," Arthur introduced the women to James and they curtsied before him.

"We did have many more servants when the Master...." Arthur hesitated and his face darkened slightly. "We manage the house quite well sir, but if extra help is required, we can certainly make enquiries. Of course, if you decide to spend a lot of time here, I would recommend a permanent cook. Mrs Ash is very busy with her other duties, but can cook for dinner parties when required, though I am sure she would find it overwhelming and terribly tiring on top of her other duties.

Tyler nodded. "Well, we'll see," he was not quite sure what else to say.

"Could you show Colonel Tyler around the rest of the house Arthur? I am sure these ladies have duties to attend to." With that, everyone moved out of the room.

As Tyler followed Banks into the wide hallway, he grabbed the older man's coat sleeve. "I can't live here," he whispered.

Sir Henry stopped and turned around. "And why not?" he asked with a puzzled look.

"Well, for a start, it's far too big for me and because er…I don't know, I just can't. It's just all so…"

"Overwhelming?"

Tyler nodded. "Yes, I suppose that is exactly what I was trying to say."

"Listen James, you don't mind if I call you James do you?" James shook his head.

"You can live here, it is yours. It is what George had wanted or he would never have bequeathed it to you. If you feel that you cannot live here, then it will be sold and you will have put the entire Ash family out onto the streets. Colonel Radcliffe was very fond of these people, and he was very reliant upon them, especially after his mother had died. They worked for both of George's parents for years and then, when they died, George kept them on." "They have nowhere else to go James." By the time he had finished speaking, he was poking Tyler in the chest.

Tyler looked at the intricately tiled floor.

"I think Arthur is waiting for us," Sir Henry said, as he turned and walked away. Tyler stood dumfounded in defeat and surprise.

Arthur gave the two men a guided tour, knowing that although Sir Henry knew the house well, he would enjoy himself by pointing out a few things that had Arthur missed. The servant smiled.

Below stairs, there was a large kitchen. A door led out into a small yard, which contained the coal cellar and laundry room. The Butler's Pantry and the wine cellar were just off the kitchen.

As the three men returned to the hall, Arthur pointed to the room which James and Henry had first entered. "That is the drawing room, and Master George always entertained in that room, but of course, you may have other plans. It leads to the library," he explained as they followed him through to the adjoining room. The library contained an ornate desk, a couple of comfortable chairs, and a square, Broadwood piano. The walls were lined from floor to ceiling with book cases, the exception being, the wall with double opening glass doors, which led on to a broad balcony, overlooking the garden. Arthur waited a few moments before leading them out of the room and across the hall. Swinging the double doors open wide, he declared, "and this is the dining room."

For the next ninety minutes, Arthur guided them from floor to floor and room to room.

As usual, the servants' quarters were on the top floor, which was actually the attic floor. Each room was spacious and had its own dormer window overlooking the street. Tyler marvelled at the fact that each room was three times larger than his own lodging room.

*Chapter 5*

Tyler moved his belongings, as meagre as they were, into his new home the next day. He still felt a little out of his depth and wondered if he could sell the place. He blushed at the thought and knew that George would probably turn in his grave and have him struck down should he should ever seriously contemplate the thought. It was infinitely better accommodation than that in which he had been living, a small garret room in lodgings just off Holborn.

As he settled in, he glanced out of his bedroom window, which overlooked the street. A few people were going about their business, and few well-dressed women, some with friends, crossed the square. A few nannies walked hand in hand with children, and carriages rumbled up and down the street.

One carriage drew up outside and Tyler went to investigate. He found two rather large men, carrying a large sea chest into the house, under Arthur's direction,

"Ah Colonel, I was just about to come and find you," the butler said.

"What on earth is happening?" Tyler questioned, eyeing the chest. He removed his coat and now stood with hands on hips with shirtsleeves rolled to his elbows.

Arthur cast a disapproving glance at Tyler's informal mode of dress. "The trunk contains Colonel George's personal belongings," he explained, quietly. "They have been kept at Sir Henry's chambers. Apparently the chest contains items, which now belong to you."

Tyler raised his eyebrows in surprise. "Would you have the men put it in my room then please Arthur?" he said. "I will investigate the contents later," he pulled Arthur to one side and slipped a guinea into his hand. "Tip them well and don't leave them alone for one moment," he whispered in the servant's ear.

"That is far too generous, Colonel." Arthur was aghast as he stared at the coin.

"I do not want them doing any damage to that chest or any of the furnishings," James whispered.

Arthur opened his mouth to speak, but then closed it. The Colonel had just indicated by his actions, that he was not the pushover, Arthur had first thought. His new employer obviously trusted no one.

"'Ow many stairs, guv'na?" one of the men asked. He fingered the coin that Arthur had handed to him, and then told him to be exceptionally careful.

"Just two short flights," Arthur replied, briskly, not giving them a chance to argue. "Come along, follow me, please," he made his way up the wide staircase, and the two labourers, struggling with the chest, followed him.

Chapter 6

Pickit was shaking Tyler hard. "Hey, mister, come on, wake up, you got to go home,"

"Where am I?" James asked, startled. He pulled himself upright.

The room was stuffy and stank of unwashed bodies, stale food and soot. "I'm the one got you away from those murdering thieves chasing you," Pickit explained. "What were they after you for anyway?"

Tyler tried to clear his head. Pickit had plied him with tea, which had been topped with gin, and Tyler wondered now, just how much of the lethal brew he had drunk.

"I went to see a couple of bare knuckle fights, and placed a few bets. I won, and one or two of the bookies were not too happy about that. They set their henchmen on to me."

"You must have taken 'em for a few guineas then."

"Aye, just a few. However, they will not miss it, just did not want me to have it for some reason. They are probably out looking for me right now."

Pickit laughed, "Nah! They will have forgotten all about you now. A few gins down their throats and you would be a distant memory. They wanted to scare you off, to make sure you do not go back. They hate big winners; it's the losers they love."

Tyler looked across at the boy. "You seem well informed."

"I used to work the crowd a bit, relieve them of a few pennies here, and a shilling or two there. So I saw what was going on."

"It sounds as though it was a lucrative line of work, why did you give it up? Or did you? "

"Oh aye, I don't go in them places anymore. A rather over-excited Bow Street Runner was watching me one night and collared me as I left. Took my money and marched me off to Bow Street."

Pickit hesitated and poured a drop of gin into a metal cup.

"And what happened?" James asked, eagerly.

"Nothing much, I waited until he relaxed his hold on me a bit, and then poked him in the eye. They can't do much to you after being poked in the eye, and then I ran off."

"So he didn't run after you?"

"Well, I kind of blinded him for a little while. Never use your measly fist when you can poke 'em in the eyes with your fingers," the lad explained.

Tyler smiled. "Remind me not to mess with you then. Anyway, he could have recognised you on the streets later."

"I suppose, but I doubt it. It was a pea souper that night, and it was very gloomy in the place where they hold the fights. It is one of the reasons I don't do it anymore. You never know when he might turn up, and I don't fancy spending any time in that Newgate hell-hole, thanks," Pickit offered the mug to James, who shook his head. "Have you been in Newgate then?"

The boy sniggered, "Yes, like the devil's own kitchen it is. Hellhole of a place, it is. Stinks like you'd never believe. I got outa there before I got the jail fever."

"Jail fever?" James questioned.

"Typhoid." Pickit looked up, "No one wants that."

Tyler stared at him for a moment, trying to decide whether the boy was telling the truth about having been inside Newgate.

"So how did you get out?"

"Bought my way out. I have a little money tucked away and one of my, well, I call him brother, brought it to the gaol and paid to get me out. That cost enough, but my so-called friend took twice as much. Still, I was free of the place and that was what mattered. I was still in the land of the living. I ain't been back, but I sure have been close," the boy laughed and slapped the table.

"It will be daylight soon, and you should get out of here before anyone around here wakes up and wants a piece of you. I'll go with you until it's safe for you to go on your own," Pickit said, as he rummaged around in the old sea chest, which he had been sitting on. He finally found a tattered coat and a pair of boots that had obviously seen better days.

Tyler recollected the events of the previous evening, which had ended with him being told countless stories by a street urchin living in a vile hovel. "Are we anywhere near Pall Mall?" he asked, trying to gather together all the events of the previous few hours.

Pickit thought for a moment, "Just a short way at a brisk walk, straight down St Martins' tis so. Is that where you live?"

"Near enough," The Colonel patted his breast pocket and the movement was not lost on the boy.

"I ain't robbed ya mister. I ain't that evil yet, that I robs me friends," he said, defiantly.

Tyler smiled. "Just a bad habit of mine that I picked up when I was in the army."

The boy scowled. "Yeah, loada fieves those Frenchies, so I heard."

"Some of the English weren't so lily-white either," Tyler retorted.

Pickit smiled, the slight now forgotten. He had found an old cloth cap that he now placed on his head at a rakish angle, and led the way out of the room.

The fog was so thick that they could barely see a hand in front of their faces. "Where the hell did this come from?" Tyler pulled his collar up against the cold, early morning air. He waited whilst Pickit locked the door and put the key, tinderbox and a new candle back in their hiding place.

The lad led the way down the rickety staircase and into the alley.

"We get this when everyone lights fires, though not usually in the middle of summer. T'aint bin much o' a summer though, has it. It's been as cold as Ode Nicks ar…"

"Yes, quite," Tyler quickly interrupted.

"Good thing I know my way around 'ere. Never know where we might end up. A good night for Low Tobies this is, so be on your guard. Drunks, vagabonds and 'god knows' who else lives around 'ere."

Tyler grimaced, as he followed the boy along the narrow passageway, he suddenly realised that the boy thought himself above those whom he was now describing. Perhaps he could have been, given different circumstances, Tyler thought.

"Aren't you cold in that thin coat?" the Colonel asked.

"Nah, it's been colder than this. It was a bad winter a couple o' years back. River iced up, it was. The Frost Fair lasted four days, and I made a good bit o' money I can tell you," Pickit chatted away amiably, as they weaved their way along the passageways, now eerily quiet in the early morning fog.

Tyler followed the boy closely as they turned into the narrow, cobbled St Martin's Lane.

"Never seen it that bad before, have you?" They could barely see the buildings either side of the lane.

"No," Tyler mumbled, his teeth chattering. "I was away, out of the country then."

"Were you fightin' 'Boney' then?"

Tyler nodded. "It seems that I've been fighting that man all my life."

"Did you ever get close to him? Did you ever meet him?" Pickit asked, eagerly.

"I could see him in the distance through my eyeglass, but I never met him. I would have run him through with my sword."

"I bet you would have, if you got close enough."

Tyler laughed. "I suppose I would, if he hadn't got me first."

"I ain't ever been out o' London, so I ain't seen too much though, hey, somebody led an elephant across the river when it was iced over. Just below Blackfriars Bridge it was. A sight for sore eyes that was, I can tell you," Pickit grinned.

Tyler blew into his cold hands. "I can imagine," he had noticed how clean Pickit's teeth were and the boy noticed him looking.

"Bones, Mista. Raw bones keep the ol' fangs sparkling. "Mother" told us that. Only, 'cos she never bought us meat you can be sure. Just bones, and I did wonder a few times who or what might have had a gnaw before they got to us."

The boy shrugged his shoulders, and Tyler thought he had seen, in that one action, some of the despair the lad had been through...was still going through.

"You ever seen an elephant?" Pickit asked, suddenly.

"Yes, a couple of times, but many years ago."

"Better than meeting Boney that was," Picket grinned. "It was bigger than anything I ever laid my eyes on."

"I'm sure it was," Tyler nodded.

Pickit came to a sudden stop and Tyler walked into him. The boy stumbled and Tyler reached out as the boy nearly fell over.

"Cor blimey Mister, nearly had me on my arse there," he was holding on to Tyler.

"Sorry, lad, are you alright?"

"I'm alright," Picket laughed, and righted his hat.

"Right, we are on Charing Cross, and Pall Mall is just a little further on, so not much further now," Pickit explained, digging his hands into his pockets.

"I think I can find my way from here."

"Are you sure, Mister? I mean, it's still a bit dodgy around these parts," Pickit looked a little worried. "There ain't any link-boys at this time o' the night to look after you."

"Link-boys?" Tyler raised his eyebrows.

"They see you home; make sure you don't get set upon," the boy explained.

Tyler looked around, but could see nothing beyond a few feet. "I'll be alright lad, not exactly crowded around here, is it?"

Pickit grinned. "Nah, people's tucked up on a night like this but, well there are others out and about. Well, at least you could hear 'em coming if there were any footpads about. If you can't see them, they can't see you."

"You probably saved my life tonight, so if you ever need anything, if you ever get into trouble or need anything at all, you just have to ask," he handed the boy a fistful of silver, part of his winnings from the night before. It had been sitting in his coat pocket, waiting for Tyler to find an opportunity to give it to the lad.

Pickit opened his mouth to speak, but Tyler put his hand up to stop him. "Do you know where Berkley Square is?" Tyler went to put his hand inside his jacket, but Pickit took hold of the soldier's arm. "I have heard of it, so I can find it."

"I have a friend who has a house in a street next to the square," Tyler gave him directions in full. "Ask for Lord Henry Banks and leave a message where I can find you. My name is Tyler. Colonel James Tyler. Can you remember that? If you can't get there yourself, send a message somehow."

"Oh aye, and who's going to take any notice of me, especially a toff?"

"These people will," Tyler assured him.

Pickit was still dubious, and gave Tyler a sullen look.

"I will make sure they know about you," the Colonel thought for a moment. "I will have a word with him, but will not say too much."

"It all sounds a bit doubtful to me."

"Believe me, everything will be alright. I am an officer and a gentleman, my word is my bond."

Pickit nodded and started to walk away. He hesitated, then took Tyler's hand and shook it again. "Be careful mister, there's a load of bad people out here, and they'll kill you for a penny." Before Tyler could speak, the lad had run off.

*Chapter 7*

James made his way through Charing Cross and on to Pall Mall. At each of the junctions, Suffolk Street, Hay Market and Market Street, he stepped lightly, aware that someone may be lurking just out of sight in the murky fog, ready to jump him at any time. Staying on the Mall, he quickened his pace until he was almost running. He had passed St James' Square and continued until he reached St James Street. His house was tucked away in a street, which was situated half way up. He ran at full steam and within minutes, he was standing outside his own front door.

He patted his pockets in search of his key, and it immediately dawned on him, that he was no longer in possession of his wallet.

"Damn the cur!" he hissed, and then he smiled at the irony of the situation.

It was obvious to him, that Pickit had lifted the wallet as they had collided. Pickit had stopped so abruptly, Tyler had walked into him, nearly knocking him off his feet, on Charing Cross

"Stupid. Stupid. Stupid!" Tyler cursed his feeble mindedness. "I should have checked then. Idiot!"

Unexpectedly, the door opened and Tyler found himself looking into the candle-lit face of Arthur Ash.

"Good morning Colonel," Arthur bowed his head slightly. "Did you have a pleasant evening?"

James tried hard not to laugh at the sight of his butler standing before him in his nightgown and cap. Arthur dressed as such, showed no embarrassment whatsoever, and was still subservient to his master.

"Arthur, what are you doing out of bed at this hour, man?"

"I have been listening for your homecoming, sir. I awoke sometime around four o'clock and, feeling a little thirsty, I went to get a glass of water. Seeing your bedroom door ajar, I realised you were not at home. I was a little worried, and thought I would go to my little sitting room and read for a while. Then after a short time, I heard a noise, came to investigate, and heard you at the front door. You were cursing, and I thought perhaps you were in trouble."

The two men had moved inside the house and Arthur locked the door as he spoke.

"Well, you can go off to bed to sleep now that I am safely home," James had to hold back the sudden need to giggle.

"Can I get you anything, sir, before I retire?" Arthur asked.

"No thank you, Arthur. I am all right; I think I am going straight to bed. You should do the same"

"Yes sir."

James made his way to the staircase. "Oh, could you please wake me at eight?"

"Most certainly, sir," Arthur nodded.

Tyler made his way up the wide staircase to his room, and as he turned into the corridor, he saw Lizzie, fully dressed, making her way down the second staircase. She faltered when she saw him.

"Oh Sir, you gave me quite a start." she blushed as she spoke.

James looked at her. "Where are you going?" he asked, frowning.

"Why, to lay the fires, sir, as I do every morning, sir," she flustered.

James searched for his pocket watch to no avail. "Damn the little devil," he mumbled.

"Sir?" Lizzie queried.

"Oh nothing. Nothing at all," he mumbled. "What time is it?"

"It's six thirty. Is everything alright sir?"

"Oh, yes. Yes, it is all right, Lizzie. Please, go on with your duties, I'm fine."

"Can I get you anything, Colonel?"

"No. Thank you anyway, Lizzie."

The girl gave a slight nod of her head and walked off along the corridor and down the stairs.

James opened the door to his room. The bed stood opposite the three windows that commandeered most of the front wall. He'd had George's sea chest moved up here, and that now stood at the foot of the bed. He still had not opened it. He needed a little more time before rummaging through his friend's personal belongings.

There was a winged armchair at the side of the fireplace, which was situated on the wall opposite the door, and a small table stood at the side of his bed. The alcoves either side of the fireplace, were furnished with shelves containing books, a couple of journals and some cavalry souvenirs, a hat, a service pistol and various other items. This room was Tyler's favourite, and he would sometimes come up here to read, once Lizzie had lit a fire after supper. He found himself at peace here, which was why he had chosen it as his room, rather than one of the many others.

He removed his coat and boots and lit a lamp, and then he pulled the drapes across the windows. It was still very foggy out there, but it was getting lighter. Dawn would have normally come earlier, but it was as if the fog had held on to the night and pushed back the daylight. He sat at the small writing desk in the corner of the room. He felt drained. It seemed to him as though he had spent an entire week on the streets of London.

He was furious, not so much with Pickit, but more with himself for trusting the thieving little tyke. How could he have been so stupid? He had always been so careful, never truly trusting anyone. That was until he had met George. From the moment they had met, he had trusted George. Still, he was always aware of the criminal fraternity on the streets of London, and acted accordingly, never inviting trouble, keeping away from river taverns, dark alleys and gin-palaces, lawless traps to the uninitiated. That was until this night. He had been tempted by the thrill of the fight, and even though he was now extremely wealthy, he just could not resist the lure of the gambling man, that had always gnawed at his insides. If he had not gone to the fight, and if he had not drunk so much gin, and if he had not...He rubbed his chin and felt the stubble beneath his fingers. He wondered whether Arthur had a steady hand and could shave him without cutting his throat.

He stood up and moved over to the nearest window. Pulling the curtain aside, he peered out at the murky pre-dawn light. He had lit only one of the lamps in this room, so no one looking over at this house would see him. It was utterly quiet, a perfect silence, and for a moment, he could not understand that silence. Why wasn't there the hustle and bustle of early morning traders, their carts clattering over the cobbles? No one was calling out or shouting their wares. No horses neighed, women screeched, and there was none of the cacophony of sounds, which he had become so familiar with, first in the Army and then around the lodgings, which he had occupied before taking up residence here.

He realised, probably for the first time, just how upper class this neighbourhood was. There were no traders and no criers. There were no drunken brawls or screams of women being molested. Just a few well-heeled people going sedately about their early morning business.

He thought about the previous evening. He could not believe that he had let the boy lead him to his hovel, and then plied him with gin and goodness knows what. Tyler wondered what he had been thinking: he must have taken leave of his senses. Yes, the lad had rescued him from his pursuers; however, it might have been a case of 'out of the pot and into the fire'. He now realised why the lad had taken hold of his arm when he had reached for his wallet. Why hadn't he insisted, and just tipped the lad and left?

There had been at least thirty guineas in the wallet, and the wallet itself must have cost as much, because he had inherited it from George, and George only ever bought the very best. The cost was not overly important though, not to Tyler. It was the fact that it had belonged to George that now niggled him. It was the same with the watch, a gold pocket watch and chain also bequeathed to him through George's estate. It had probably been a family heirloom, handed down amongst the Radcliffe family through the years, and now Tyler had allowed it be taken, like a rattle from a baby. The more he thought about it the angrier he became.

He paced the room, stopping occasionally to glance out of the windows at some activity, which was taking place in the Square. He was not sure who he blamed the most, himself for putting his trust in a street urchin, thief and vagabond, or Pickit for taking advantage of his vulnerability.

"Just wait until I find you my lad, and I will. You will wish you had never crossed me," Tyler promised. He lay down on the bed and he closed his eyes. A few seconds later, he was snoring gently.

Chapter Eight

The boy gasped when he realised when he saw the contents of the wallet. He was looking at the pile of money before him and, even though he could count, he could not count that much. He began to sweat, even though his hovel was cool and on the point of becoming extremely cold. He had used the last of his wood and coal the previous evening, when he had brought the soldier back, so there was no chance of building a fire. He wondered what "Mother" would have said upon seeing this little lot. He grinned. "Even if she were still with us, she would not have got her grubby hands on this lot," he said to himself, stuffing the money back into the leather purse.

He examined the pocket watch and, as he opened it, he saw the inscription in beautiful copperplate writing. Pickit could count to some degree, but read he could not. The writing, although meaning nothing to him, probably meant an awful lot to the soldier, he thought.

The lad sat down on the wooden crate and pondered his ill-gotten gains. Had the watch been presented for an act of bravery? Had it belonged to a beloved relative? Perhaps a sweetheart had given it as a love token. Whatever the reason, he now wanted to give the watch back, but how, without giving the money back too? This was a situation very alien to him, and he was not sure how to handle it. "Hock it, you stupid idiot." He ran his hand through his thick, filthy hair. "It's bound to be worth a few pennies." He felt uneasy: there was something about the watch that did not sit quite right with him. Pickit did not want it, he was regretting ever having set eyes on it, and now he could not wait to off-load it. He could not hang around the Strand in the hope of seeing a friendly fence. If the soldier just happened to be in the vicinity and spotted him, it would surely be the end of Pickit, which was another reason he had to give this little lot back. The Colonel was the type of man who frequented the lowly places and docklands of London, and in time, the two of them would meet again, the lad did not give a hoot about his own chances, when pitted against the might of man who had fought in the Peninsula Wars and come out the other side, unscathed.

He rubbed his forehead and tried to think of the name of the man the Colonel had mentioned, and also the place the soldier had told him about. He could take the whole lot there, and scarper sharpish. There would be no need to explain, just give that stupid...Pickit thought for a moment. He could not remember the name of the soldier's friend. After a few moments, he thumped the rickety table in despair. He had not been taking too much notice when the soldier had told him where he could be found. At that time, Pickit was in possession of the wallet and the watch, and only wanted to get away before the soldier discovered his losses.

A few hours later, he awoke to find that he had fallen asleep at the table, his forehead resting on his folded arms. He sat up and yawned. Then he remembered.

"Berkley Square," he whispered, and then smiled.

"Banks, Henry Banks. That's who I have to see," he grinned and clapped his hands.

Pickit shivered, now feeling really, really cold. He would go out and get some provisions, wood, coal, food, especially food, yes, and some gin to help him through the next few hours, while he pondered his plight.

Opening the trunk, he rummaged around for something half-decent to wear, and found a pair of worn, tan leather breeches and a dark-coloured cropped riding jacket. He did not own a pair of stockings, so chose a tattered pair of boots without holes in the soles. He also chose a shirt, that had at one time, been white, but had now become a dirty yellow, with age. It had a ruffle at the neck, so he would not need a cravat, and the colour of the shirt would just about match the colour of the breeches.

"Not exactly the Prince Regent, but, we'll do," he sniggered, looking at his reflection in a grimy piece of silvered glass. He had already dunked his mop of straw like hair into a bowl of freezing water, and had plastered it down to his head with his hands. Now that it had dried, most of it sprang out at odd angles over his ears. With a final glance at the glass, he let himself out of the room. Making sure no one was about; he hid the key in a new hiding place, as he had stupidly allowed the soldier to see all his secret hiding places.

Pickit patted his breast pocket, assuring himself that the wallet and watch were safe. He had finally remembered where Tyler's friend resided, and was now making his way to Berkley Square hopefully to find someone by the name of Banks. The lad had kept a little money from the purse, assured that Tyler could would not know, to the penny, how much the wallet contained. He did not think of it as stealing, but more like recompense for saving the Colonel's life.

He walked purposefully down through the narrow alley. At some point in the past two or three hours, there had been a shower of rain. The cobbles were wet and slippery, and Pickit took care where he trod, but did not slow. He was hoping that the rain would not return, as he did not want to arrive soaked to the skin.

A few people who knew him, asked where he was going, all dressed up like a toff, or jested that he was off to see his fancy woman. He just laughed and dismissed their comments.

"You orf to see the old King then, Pickit? Collecting yer in'eritence early, are ya?" one old tar asked, laughing. "Nah, e'd ne'er get a crown on that mop o' 'air," another retorted.

"Neh mind 'is mop, it's 'is 'ead that would be a problem," an old crone joined in.

Pickit laughed and waved them away. As rough as these people were, they were the nearest things to friends as could be, in this area. They would fight and squabble amongst themselves but would stand shoulder to shoulder at the first sign of trouble from 'outsiders'.

A child, skinny and filthy, wearing an assortment of rags, observed him as he traversed the slimy gutters. Pickit searched his coat and then tossed a coin to the urchin. The child caught it and examined it with squinting eyes. Squealing with delight, he ran off.

A short while later, Pickit crossed from St Martin's Lane up to Coventry Street and on to Piccadilly. Not having the exact address, Pickit knew he would have to start making enquiries. This was the part of his quest that made him nervous. He eventually arrived at Berkley Square and began asking directions from anyone who would deign to stop and talk to him.

He felt the niggling signs of a headache and the rumble of his stomach, both caused by lack of food. He should have eaten earlier but he had wanted to get this finished. He slowed and started looking at buildings. He did recognise some words, but he did not think that his limited knowledge would help him.

He saw a couple of smartly dressed men heading his way.

"'Scuse me, gents. Could ya direct me to Mista Banks?" Pickit asked, nervously.

They stopped and eyed him cautiously. "And why would you want to see him?" the taller of the two asked.

"I have messages for him," Pickit replied.

"You can tell us and we will make sure he gets them," the men looked at each other.

Pickit knew that look, he had seen it often enough. "Well, ta for yer 'elp, but I need to see him for meself," he backed away.

"Now lad, come on. Don't you go off like that. We'll take you to him," the tall one tried to take hold of the boy's arm.

Pickit dodged out of the way and walked swiftly along the road towards the Square. He listened for their footsteps, then when he thought he was at a safe distance, he turned slightly and glanced over his shoulder. They were standing there watching him. He continued on, occasionally glancing back until he saw the two men walking in the opposite direction.

Grabbing some black painted railings, which fronted a four-storey house, he stood for a moment to catch his breath. He had realised just how scared he had been, talking to those two men. Though they were dressed in expensive looking clothes, and their boots were so highly polished that he could see his face in them, he knew that they were not gentry in the true meaning of the word. They were out looking to fleece anyone gullible enough to fall for their wily ways.

"Oi! Get your filthy hands off the railings," Pickit nearly fell over with fright. He looked over to where a strange looking youth stood, on the steps of the house. Pickit quickly let go of the railings and wiped his hands on his breeches.

"Oh sorry," Pickit said, apologetically. "I was just catching me breath."

"You'll be catching the back of my hand if you don't clear off," the youth started to close the door.

"No, wait!" Picket called.

"What?" the youth snapped.

"Do you know a Mr Banks?" He asked.

"And why do you want to know?" the youth looked intrigued.

Pickit sighed, loudly. "I have something for him," he was becoming tired of the stupid questions.

"I bet you do. Sod off!" the youth announced, and was about to close the door.

No, wait," Pickit pleaded. "I met a Colonel last night and he left some things behind which I need to give back. He had mentioned a Mr Banks on Berkeley Street. Now, do you know him or not?" Pickit was losing his composure and now wished that he had not bothered coming here.

The youth held up his hand. "Wait there. I'll be back in a minute, and don't touch anything."

A few moments later, an older man dressed in a black frock coat, black stockings and patent leather shoes with silver buckles, appeared on the steps.

"How can I help you?" he enquired, looking at Pickit.

"I'm looking for a Mr Banks. No, that ain't right," Pickit frowned and tried to concentrate. "Ah yeah, it's Sir Banks. Do you know of him?"

The man's eyebrows rose. "Then you have found us. Won't you please come in?"

Pickit frowned. "I won't if you don't mind. I just want to leave this."

He handed the wallet and the watch, now wrapped in a piece of grubby linen, to the gentleman. "The Colonel dropped this, he dropped it he did and I brought it back for him. He talked about you, so I thought I'd bring it here."

Sir Henry looked puzzled. "I am sure Colonel Tyler would like to thank you himself. I could take you there."

"Naw, I wouldn't want to bother 'im with all that. Anyway, I see you're a proper gent, you'll see he gets it then?"

Sir Henry Smiled. "You can count on it."

"Yeah, well. You are 'im ain't ya?"

"I surely am, young man." He pointed to a black plaque on the wall. The plaque was embossed with gold letters, which Pickit could not read.

With that, Pickit turned on his heel and ran off in the direction from where he had come..

Banks looked down at the wallet and the rag-encased watch, and then leant over the railings to watch as the boy ran off towards Charring Cross.

Chapter Nine

Once Pickit had reached the Strand, he felt more at ease. His headache was now throbbing and his stomach thought that his throat had been cut. He headed towards a tavern on Craven Street. Here he could eat and drink his fill whilst watching the activity of the shipping, and the comings and goings of the dockers, warehouse men and others who were going about their daily lives.

He sat by a window in the corner of the room, from where he could see the Thames and, by turning his head the other way, he could see the door that opened onto the Strand. He ordered a huge bowl of stew, half a loaf of bread and a pint of gin. The whole lot cost him sixpence. He gave the serving girl a shilling piece and told her to keep the change. She almost fainted, then returned every five minutes to see if there was anything else he required. In the end, he snapped and told her to clear off.

A few minutes later, an elderly man of about fifty years, wearing the remnants of a soldier's uniform sat on a stool opposite Pickit. He sported a woollen cap with a feather in the band, on top a mass of white hair, which curled around his ears.

"What do you want?" Pickit growled, stuffing another spoonful of the stew into his hungry mouth.

The man laughed. "Oh, my dear boy. Now why would you think I would want anything?"

"You usually do. Now sod off, you're stinking the place out!"

"How could you be so cruel to a feeble, old man? I am your friend. I think of you as my own, my very own dear child," the man rambled, theatrically waving his arm in the air.

Pickit spluttered and a mouthful of gravy landed on the table.

"Your own?" Pickit hissed. "It wasn't so long ago, that you plied me with gin until I was almost senseless, then tried to sell me to a slave trader."

The man laughed. "A misunderstanding. Just a misunderstanding, my boy."

Pickit glowered and continued to eat.

The be-whiskered man held up his empty tankard. "Just to show there are no hard feelings on your part, I will let you buy me a pint of gin."

"Buy your own gin, and whilst you're at it, go and sit somewhere else, you stink," Pickit used the last of his bread to mop the bowl.

The old man, with a menacing look, leant across the table and took hold of Pickit's arm. "You have money Pickit, I seen it. I saw how much you gave that wench, so you can buy me a drink," he hissed, through blackened teeth.

"I did have money, but I have just spent it on my dinner, and gave a few pennies to the serving girl. If you don't let go of my arm, I will pull yours out of its socket and knock the rest of your teeth out with it."

The man let go and roared with laughter. "You have no sense of humour my boy, none at all."

Pickit shoved his tankard towards the old soldier. "You can finish that if you like, there may be just enough to wet your whistle...or choke you. I have other things to tend to."

He left the table and the old man gulped the dregs of his tankard. As he approached the door, he gave the wench, now serving other customers, a friendly slap on her ample backside.

"You keep yer filthy hands off me arse, ya dirty little bugger," she gave him a friendly shove out of the door and Pickit laughed loudly.

Feeling better than he had all day, he made his way along the Strand and on to St Martin's Lane. A few yards further up the narrow road, he came to a coal merchant. A little while later after haggling over the price, the coal merchant's boy, dragging a trolley full of wood and coal behind him, followed Pickit, who strode out, leading the way.

Pickit had dismissed the coal merchant's lad, but only after, he had promised the lad three pence to stand guard over his precious load while he changed his clothes. He then humped it up the three floors to his loft. Only then had he let the young lad leave, happily clutching the money.

Though Pickit was skinny, he was wiry and quite strong and, after a little while, the sacks were safely stashed away. He estimated that the fuel would last him most of the coming winter.

Now a fire was blazing in the hearth, and there was a large, brass kettle of water hanging from a hook just inside the chimney. Tonight he would have a strip wash in hot water, make some tea, and tuck into the bread rolls and slices of ham topped off with cake, which he had purchased before buying the coal and wood. Tonight he would be warm, clean and well fed and he would sleep like a baby. His conscience was clear now that he had returned the wallet and watch, hopefully to their rightful owner.

Tomorrow night he would be earning a few more pounds, once the warehouse owner came back from his overseas excursions. There would be crates of tobacco and silks and other exotic goods, and barrels of spirits, all to be stored in the cavernous rooms below Pickit's loft. All this would take place under cover of darkness.

Of course, as well as payment in cash, he would also receive a couple of bottles of spirits, a pound of tea and other goodies that would last him a while. It was all part of his wages, as was the free accommodation, such as it was. Pickit was well satisfied with his lot.

He stoked the fire, and the water in the large kettle began to bubble. Stripping off his clothes, he took the kettle and poured most of the contents into an old porcelain basin. He spent the next fifteen minutes or so, cleaning himself and washing his hair. He dried himself in front of the blazing fire, and then donned some clean clothes.

When he had finished, he sat at his makeshift table and poured himself a generous helping of gin, and thought of the events of the day as he sipped. He wondered if he would ever have the chance of a better life. "You can bet on it, my lad," he whispered, as he gulped down the last drop of gin.

Chapter Ten

The house was quiet after the hustle and bustle of the morning, and James took the opportunity to catch up on some correspondence. Sitting at a small desk in the drawing room, he wrote to his few friends informing them of his change of address, though not of his change of circumstance. The last thing he wanted was a load of hangers-on. Engrossed as he was in his thoughts, he did not hear the carriage pull up, and nor did he hear Arthur answer the front door. Therefore, he was somewhat startled when Arthur knocked lightly and opened the drawing room door.

"I'm sorry to disturb you, Colonel, but Sir Henry has called to see you," Arthur bowed slightly and handed a calling card to his master.

James got up and put the quill back in the inkwell. "Thank you Arthur, please show him in."

"James, my dear sir, I do hope I am not disturbing you," Sir Henry held out his hand and James shook it, warmly.

"No, not at all, I was just writing a few letters, nothing too demanding or urgent," he pointed to a chair near the window, which overlooked the lawn.

"Arthur, could you bring some tea please. I hope that is all right for you, Sir Henry."

"Yes please, Arthur. That would be very nice,"

Sir Henry handed the small case he carried, to James.

"I believe the contents of this belong to you," he said, by way of an explanation.

James looked puzzled.

Sir Henry, enjoying himself, shifted in his seat, making himself more comfortable

"A young man of questionable circumstances presented himself in front of my house this morning, frightening poor Fielding half to death. He asked for me by name, but Fielding was rather suspicious, for the young man looked somewhat unkempt. Anyway, eventually, Fielding came to me and said there was someone asking for me. When I presented myself, a young man handed me the contents of that case. He would not come in or explain himself to me. He did explain however, that you had left these things behind, though behind where, I have yet to determine." He frowned and shifted in his seat.

James tried to hide his amusement and opened the case. He uttered an audible gasp when he saw what it contained.

"He said you left them behind, though he didn't say where." Sir Henry continued, probing for any clue as to what James had been up to.

James was so surprised he could not think of what to say.

"I would have recognised the watch anywhere," Sir Henry continued. "George's mother had given it to George when he was still young, a birthday present I do believe, though I have a sneaking suspicion that she had actually bought it, or more probably, had it made for Lord Radcliffe. I presume he had died before she could present it to him."

The door opened and Arthur entered with a tray. Deftly, he moved things aside from the table and placed the tray on it. "Shall I pour, sir?" Arthur asked.

James smiled and nodded. Neither Sir Henry nor Tyler spoke again until Arthur had left the room.

"When I returned home last night, I thought I had been robbed, as I no longer had these items about my person," James explained. "These items must have fallen out of my pocket at some time during the evening. Usually, I'm so careful."

"Easily done, though I am surprised that the boy decided to return them. I do not know how he knew where to bring them."

"Ah! I might be able to answer that." James smiled and took a sip of his tea.

"I was in a tavern talking to an ex-soldier friend of mine. We were at Waterloo together, a grand chap, frightened of nothing. I did mention you, and of course, how kind you had been. Naturally, I did not go into any details of my good fortune. At one point, Parker, my friend, did ask where you resided though I only said St James' Park. He said then that he did know of you."

"You should really be more careful James, not all are as honest and trustworthy as the young man who returned your items."

James nodded, trying not to shudder. "I am aware of that, Sir Henry."

"I wouldn't carry as much money either," the older man advised.

"I don't usually, but I'd had some luck with a wager."

"A gambling man, hey?" Banks winked

"Not usually," James laughed. "The odds were just a little too tempting. I won't be going there again though, you can rest assured."

"Oh, I nearly forgot." Sir Henry clapped his hands together. "My dear wife has organised a dinner party for Saturday, are you free or do you have a prior engagement? I hope you are free. My dear Sarah would be distraught if you could not attend."

James thought for a moment. "As far as I know, I have nothing planned, so I would be delighted."

"Eight p.m. then," Sir Henry handed over a small, gold embossed card which showed the time and date of the event. "Oh, and if you could wear your dress uniform, it would certainly keep the ladies happy."

James laughed again. "I had better get Arthur to remove the blood stains then."

Sir Henry looked horrified until James burst out laughing again.

Once he had seen Sir Henry to his carriage, he returned to the house and went in search of Arthur. He found him out in the scullery, polishing James's boots.

"Arthur, do you think Mrs Ash could wash and iron my best white shirt and could you press my uniform and polish the buttons? I will see to the rest myself."

Arthur smiled. "It is all in hand, sir, and being taken care of right now."

"Thank you, Arthur."

"Just a little point, sir, if you don't mind my saying," Arthur hesitated.

"Go on," James urged.

"A small token for the wife of your host wouldn't go amiss. I do happen to know the lady in question is very partial to earrings, especially if they contain rubies."

"Thank you, Arthur. I shall keep that in mind."

"Oh sir. I think you will want a carriage for the evening. Forgive me for speaking out of turn."

"Yes Arthur, go on."

"I know it isn't far to Sir Henry's, but, apart from the fact that it might be raining, I wouldn't advise walking that far in your dress boots."

Tyler laughed. "A good point, Arthur. A carriage it is then."

Tyler returned to the drawing room, picked up the wallet and examined the contents. He did not know if all the money was there, as he had no idea exactly how much had been in there to begin with. He was sure that his new friend Pickit would have helped himself to a few, or perhaps even more than a few shillings. However, James did not resent it at all. He appreciated the fact that wallet and the watch had been returned with the minimum of fuss.

There was a tap at the door and Arthur appeared.

Tyler looked up.

"Sorry to bother you, sir, but Lizzie would like to know if you would like her to light a fire in your room tonight. There is an awful chill in the air, and by this evening, it will be so much colder."

"I think that would be a good idea. I shall be retiring early, anyway and may read for a while. A fire would be most welcome."

"I'll make sure you have everything you need, sir. I believe you enjoy a brandy after dinner. I will arrange that also."

James smiled, "I'll take one up to bed with me also. Just to help me sleep."

Arthur bowed. "I'm sure it will, sir," he closed the door behind him.

James smiled to himself. "I could get used to this," he mumbled.

During his army career, a batman was always there to take care of his uniform. A batman would also take care of your equipment and your arms whether it be sword, rifle or any other weaponry you had at your disposal.

In all those years, no one had ever been as attentive as Arthur. George's family had chosen well. Tyler did not know yet whether he was accepted, resented or just tolerated by his inherited servants. He was hoping that they liked him, as he liked them. He realised that time would tell, and hoped that they would accept him and his sometimes unorthodox ways.

James Tyler had realised long ago that he was way out of George's class, being somewhat rough and ready at times. However, he knew no other way, and although not actually dragged out of the gutter, he had not been brought up in the way George had been. Still, he was happy with his lot, and George's generosity had eliminated all worry of how Tyler was going to pay his way through life after the Army.

Tyler spent the afternoon on household accounts with Arthur, and sometimes with Mrs Ash also. Arthur proved a mine of information, knowing the price of everything from a lump of coal to the cost of a pair of fine thoroughbred horses.

They agreed on a household allowance, James proving to be a little more than generous, and finally put the ledgers away just after six p.m.

By the time Tyler had finished dinner, it was just after eight p.m. Lizzie had laid and lit a fire whilst he was dining, and he then made his way up to his room.

He stood at the windows, looking out over the street. It was still light outside, although the fog was beginning to descend. This did not deter the foot traffic or those riding in carriages on their way to dine, or to the theatre. The area was always quiet, as the street did not lead anywhere, so there was no traffic

James walked over to the chair by the side of the fireplace and picked up his book. He thought he might read for a while, but as much as he tried to lose himself in the pages, his mind kept wandering to thoughts of Pickit and why the lad had returned the wallet and watch. Perhaps the inscription on the watch made it too hot to handle, but the money...why had he returned the money. Tyler could not make rhyme or reason of it. Still, he did not resent it at all. The boy had helped him in his hour of need, without thought of his own safety and well-being. The money was nothing to James now, but it probably meant the difference between eating and starving to the lad. No, James did not have any regrets. He just counted his blessings and his own good fortune.

Chapter 11

As Tyler was sitting in his comfortable armchair in front of a roaring fire, trying to concentrate on his book, Pickit was opening up the warehouse for two rather burly men. The alley was almost pitch dark, and even if there had been a full moon, it could not have penetrated this part of London due to the smoke from hundreds of chimney. The smog now blanketed everything and the visibility was down to about ten yards.

"Are things still alright for you lad?" the man nodded towards the loft.

"No bother, just a bit cold at nights, but I get used to it, Mister Scrimms."

"No trouble then?" Said the other man who Pickit knew as Barley.

"Nah, not at all. Thanks for asking," Pickit grinned.

Scrimms took hold of the lad's arm. "Look at ya. I have seen 'roaches with more meat on 'em than you have on you. Ya should take more care o' yo'self."

"Aw' leave the lad alone, Jack. He is a-growin' up, bound to be a bit skinny fer a bit. He'll fill out soon enough."

Jack Scrimms grimaced. "I don't want folks a-sayin I don't look afta me lads, when you knows full well I do."

"I'm alright, Mister Scrimms. Mister Barley is right, I'm just a growin'."

"Well, in that case then, I'll up your wage a bit. Pay for all that extra grub you are going to need in your belly. Skinny arse that you are."

Barley laughed. "I never thought I'd see the day. Well I never, Scrimms being generous."

Scrimms glowered at his partner. "Who else would you trust if anything happened to him?" He pointed his thumb in Pickit's direction. "He's our best lad and I'd trust him with my life. He's worth a few more pennies, ain't ya, Pickit lad?"

Pickit grinned and nodded.

"Come on, Jack, let's get ourselves movin', or else morning will be here afore we know it," Barley knew his friend was heavily indebted to Pickit; the lad had been looking after the warehouse for years and knew who to employ, how many and when. Both men well and truly trusted the lad.

Jack Scrimms scowled at Pickit. "You heard him, git movin."

Pickit moved into the warehouse and over to the far wall. He spoke in a whisper, and suddenly fifteen or sixteen youths moved out into the pool of light shining from the lantern, which Pickit was holding just above his head.

"Do everything you're told and you will be paid well. Tell anyone about this and you'll end up in an alley with yer throats cut," Pickit hissed, through clenched teeth. By the time he had manoeuvred the boys to the now wide-open double doors, he could hear the faint clop of horses' hooves.

"Not a sound from any of ya. Just do as yer told." He led some of the group out into the alley as the first pony arrived. "Unload each pony and take the crates to the back of the room as I described before. Only two of ya to a horse. Any barrels should be rolled to that side," he indicated the right and side of the building.

One lad started whistling some unidentifiable ditty and Pickit clipped his ear. "For gawd's sake be quiet, can't ya? Are you tryin' to wake the dead?"

A short time later, all the ponies had been unloaded and sent back to whence they came. At one point, three youths dragged a laden cart up the alley to the warehouse, and by the time they arrived at the double doors, sweat had trickled down their filthy, dirt-encrusted skin, leaving water trail patterns on their arms, legs and faces. Jack Scrimms threw a pile of gold coins in their direction and the boys spent the next few minutes squabbling over the money, until Scrimms booted the lads out of the way.

"Clear off, you 'orrible lot, and say anything to anybody an' I'll cut thee bloody tongues out!" Jack placed a well-aimed boot on the backside of the nearest lad. The boy squealed, more in shock than in pain, and ran after the others.

"Right, gents, is that all, then?" Pickit asked.

"Aye' tis so, lad. For tonight anyway. We will be havin' a big delivery in a couple of weeks, so let's hope we can shift this lot before then, hey?" Scrimms laughed and handed Pickit a pouch. "They were a good bunch o' lads tonight, we'll use 'em again,"

Pickit nodded. "It's all in hand, Mister Scrimms."

Scrimms patted the boy's shoulder. "Keep this snippet of information tight to your chest lad, but we might be moving to more salubrious premises in the near future, and you may be moving to better lodgings. Business is good and getting better. So, as long as the Runners know nothing about it, we are all going to be a tad richer than we are now."

Pickit nodded. "You know me, gov'. I'll keep me eyes peeled and my mouth shut."

"Good lad. Anything you need?" Scrimms asked.

"Nah, I'm alright. Looking forward to moving though. It's mighty cold up there, never known anything like this. I ain't looking forward to winter if this weather is anything to go by." the boy rubbed his hands together.

Scrimms looked thoughtful. "Well you're a good lad, and I need you on the premises, so if you like, you can move down to the second floor. There is a room at the front overlooking the alley. The doorway is around the side there, under the stairway. It is supposed to be an office or something, but I won't need it. There is a fireplace and a small window, and the place needs fumigating, but it is probably better than what you live in now. Anyway, It is yours if you want it," he hesitated. "I trust you not to bring any of your kind here, though. I do not care how well you know 'em, keep 'em at arm's length. Don't get too close to anyone, lad, they'll stab you in the back one day, you mark my words."

Pickit grinned. "No worries, Mister Scrimms. I don't have friends, and don't need 'em either."

Scrimms smiled. "That's good then," he played with a bunch of keys, trying to prise one off the brass ring. He handed a small, rusty key to Pickit. "Do not lose the bloody thing. It's the only one I have." Pickit took hold of the key and tied it to the warehouse key, which he kept hidden in his boot. Scrimms patted the lad on the shoulder, and without another word, he marched off to join his counterpart. Pickit danced a little jig, and then saw two scruffy urchins sucking their thumbs and watching him. He stamped his foot and they scurried away. He did not need anyone knowing his business.

Chapter 12

He waited until midnight, and then quietly set about moving his meagre belongings down two floors to his new address. He had spent some time removing the vermin, and scrubbing the place, and he had even found a new pallet for his bed. He had bought some bedding and other items from an old hag wheeling a dilapidated cart, loaded with cast offs and rags, down on the Strand. He had sorted the cleanest and least ragged, and after haggling for a good fifteen minutes, finally carried his goods away.

Pickit looked around his new lodging. It bigger than his old room and, being in the middle of the warehouse, a lot less draughty. He had cleaned the small windowpanes, none of which were cracked, and had hung a couple of sacks over a pole, which gave him a little privacy.

A fire was blazing in the grate, and there was a hot meal of stew and a pint of gin on his table. A real table, albeit a little rickety, which he had scrounged off some old hag for half a penny. He still sat on wooden crates, but he had clean bedding, a few clean clothes, wood and even coal for a fire. There was plenty of water available, which could be pumped up from the warehouse below.

He sat and ate his stew, all the while counting the stacks of coins, which were piled up in rows in front of him. He was rich to the tune of almost fifty guineas. He had more tucked away in safe places, but he had never counted the entire hoard. In the morning, he would find a safe and secure place to hide it all. He wanted it close by, and somewhere where it could not accidently be found. He wondered if his floorboards would yield a hiding place, or would the floorboards just be the ceiling of the expansive warehouse below. He would investigate in the morning.

James Tyler crossed his mind, and Pickit wondered if the man's belongings had been returned to him. He could not really see why not. After all, Mr Binks, Banks or whatever his name was, seemed to be a thoroughly proper gent and obviously not short of a few pennies, going by the appearance of the place in which he lived..

He felt the need to find out where the Colonel lived and had secreted himself in some shrubbery, hoping that it wouldn't be too long before someone would lead him to the soldier's home. He was not about to be disappointed, as after a short while, Sir Henry appeared and started walking briskly along the street.

Pickit kept his distance, making sure that there was no one watching. He kept to the shadows, his hands tucked in his pockets. His face pointed forward as if he was strolling, but with some purpose.

A short time later, Banks finally stopped in front of an imposing looking residence and rapped lightly on the door with his cane. Within moments, he was admitted. Pickit sat on a bench under the shade of an oak tree, watched and waited.

He had just closed his eyes when he heard a familiar voice. Looking towards the building, he saw Banks about to leave the house and then the Colonel stepped out and shook the older man's hand. Pickit smiled to himself, and after waiting for a good while, he left the safety of the tree and made his way home.

In the morning, he was off to see an old friend. Tobias Fowler, thief, tooler, highwayman, and of late, attempted murderer. He was on a prison hulk on the Thames, awaiting deportation to lands unknown. The man was to be moved to a convict ship on the morrow, ready to be transported to his place of banishment. The only reason they had not hanged him was, that he had acted in self-defence. A witness had seen the whole thing and said so to the court. It came to pass, that the witness held a long-standing feud with the victim, and was more than happy that Toby had given the man a thrashing, and therefore spoke in the defence of the accused in the courtroom.

Tobias or Toby as Pickit called him, was the closest thing to a friend the boy had, having struck up the friendship when they were attacked by the mud larks down on the muddy shore of the Thames, one dark night. Standing back-to-back, Pickit and Toby had fended off their assailants, and from that moment, they had been firm friends, though as such, each lived his own life and they only met up occasionally for a drink or a meal. They would dine in one of the many eating-houses along the waterfront, where they would try to outdo each other with stories of their exploits.

It was quite by accident that Pickit had found out that Toby was in Newgate and awaiting trial. At the first opportunity, the lad had managed to visit his friend, armed with coins, food and gin, goods that would make Toby's life in shackles, just a little easier.

Both the prisoner and Pickit were surprised when Toby's sentence was commuted to a deportation order, to a land neither had ever hear of...New Holland.

That day had arrived. In the morning, Pickit would collect a bundle of clothes and food, which were being kept for him by Jack Scrimms's wife. He would add some money and take it all to his friend. It would help to keep him alive on the long sea voyage, and the money would also be useful for bribes. Pickit would have to get there early, as Toby was being moved to the convict ship at eight a.m. The ship would sail on the high tide at about ten a.m. Pickit would be allowed only a few minutes with Toby. Normally, only the closest of relatives would be allowed to see a prisoner prior to sailing, but Pickit had paid the bribe, and he would see his friend off on his long journey.

Chapter 13

It had only just started raining when James left his house; however, by the time he reached Sir Henry's residence it was raining heavily. As he stepped from the carriage, a footman of Jamaican origin appeared, carrying a large umbrella. "Good evening, Colonel. My name is Joseph; let me escort you into the house."

The wide hallway, which James entered, was warm and inviting, combating the bone aching, damp clutches of the cold night outside.

"Ah James, come in, my boy, come in. I have people here who are looking forward to meeting you. And might I add sir, you do look rather splendid." Sir Henry stood back and looked at the young man in the uniform of an Officer in the Ist Life Guards. He wore a red tunic with a white sash, black pants with a red stripe down the side, and shining black boots on his feet. At his left hip, a gleaming sword hung in its scabbard. James carried his shako under his left arm.

"I hope Arthur managed to remove all the blood stains," James whispered, conspiratorially.

Sir Henry laughed and guided the Colonel towards the drawing room. "Come on, James, I'll introduce you. Joseph, please take the Colonel's sword and hat, we do not wish to frighten the ladies now, do we?"

As the two men walked through the double doors and into the drawing room, James saw the most beautiful woman he had ever laid eyes on. He felt his face redden. "Ah, Isobel, this is Colonel James Tyler. James, this is my daughter," James bowed and took hold of her outstretched hand, his lips brushing lightly across her fingers.

Throughout the meal, James had felt slightly uncomfortable, as, every time he looked up, Isobel was looking at him. Her mother Sarah, Lady Banks, an older version of her beautiful daughter, had treated him like a long lost son. She was charming and witty, and interested to hear all about him. James found her quite amenable and felt totally at ease in her company.

"I am rather interested in the Colonel's exploits alongside our dear Duke of Wellington," Sarah smiled at her husband, "You don't mind do you dear?" Sir Henry smiled and shook his head. "I think we can break with tradition on this one occasion as I am sure the gentlemen present would like to hear about it first-hand so to speak."

There was much nodding of heads and mumbles of assent.

James coughed lightly and took a sip of wine. "I really don't think it's a suitable subject for mixed company."

Sarah laughed. "We aren't as meek as you men think we are," the other women in the room nodded in agreement.

James blushed, and then glanced at Sir Henry. The older man winked and nodded.

He glanced over at Isobel sitting opposite him and saw something in her eyes, which unnerved him somewhat. He cast his eyes down and took hold of the intricately cut crystal glass but did not drink.

"I lost a very dear friend in the battle and it is still raw. It is far too gruesome to relate in mixed company however, I am sure that you are already aware, thousands of men lost their lives in the worst possible ways." James said, looking at the ruby red liquid he swirled in his glass.

"I remember reading about it," Lord Graham said, nodding, "a blood bath, by all accounts."

"My husband could probably relate the whole thing, being the historian he is," Lady Graham smiled, "he read every news print he could acquire that mentioned Lord Nelson, Napoleon, the Duke of Wellington or Waterloo."

There was laughter around the room.

"Ah yes, but if I had been younger, I would have been there," he grinned, broadly. "And if that darned horse hadn't taken my kneecap off when I was younger, I would have been with Nelson at Trafalgar."

"Never mind, dear, you are at least here." Lady Graham patted her husband's arm.

"Thank goodness for the London Gazette. Sorry James, never mind me." Lord Graham smiled, wistfully.

"Where were you during the battle, Major, I am sure you can at least tell us that?" Isobel smiled, but James was aware of the derision in her voice.

James shrugged his shoulders. "There is a farm by the name of La Haye Sainte. It stands in the valley below a crest. Wellington decreed that the Germans should occupy it.

Below a second crest, stands another farm, the La Belle Alliance, which the French occupied, and were using as a headquarters. The small chateau of Hougoumont stood before the extreme right of the Allied position.

Wellington thought that the chateau should be used for some of our troops."

James felt hot and sweat bubbled out on his brow. It was not just the warmth of the room; it was also the memory of that terrible day. He and George, side by side, the cannonade assaulting the walls of the chateau, then George's headless body, lying in the filth. James blinked and swallowed hard, feeling nauseous as he saw it all again. He was about to take another sip of wine when Lady Sarah stood up.

"Could we please have a window open? It is terribly stuffy in here. Fielding, open the doors please." She walked around to where James was sitting and poured him a glass of water from a carafe. She squeezed his shoulder gently and he smiled up at her.

"Are you alright, James? Can you go on, or would you rather not?" she asked, softly.

"Are you feeling a little better James?" Sir Henry asked.

"I'm feeling much better now, thank you, Sir Henry. Talking about that terrible day just brought it all back."

James gave a wry smile. "During any battle, there is always the man who stands out. Someone who gives that little bit extra.

During the afternoon, when the supply of ammunition in the chateau was becoming critically low, Sergeant Fraser of the 3rd Guards, travelled up to the main line. No one had any idea how he had managed to get through, as the French were everywhere. Sergeant Fraser returned with a wagon of cartridges, riding the horses like some demented banshee through the enemy assembled in their hundreds. They looked at him as if he was some spectral harbinger of everything unholy. Those of us in the chateau were cheering him on.

"Having managed to open the gates, he drove the wagon through, barely stopping in time, before crashing into one of the buildings. We managed to close the gates before the French had time to come to their senses and clamber in. His bravery enabled us to continue with the defence of the chateau."

A footman now offered to fill his glass and James nodded. Other servants followed the footman's lead and replenished everyone else's glasses.

"The details would only bore you to tears but suffice to say, Wellington appeared on the skyline sometime later. He waved his hat to give the signal for a general attack, in pursuit of the French troops who were fleeing for their lives. Three battalions of the Old Guard fought to the end, and this enabled the Emperor to escape from the battlefield. The Allied troops, including the Prussians, closed in.

The fighting continued even as dusk fell, but then between nine and ten p.m., Wellington and Blücher met near Napoleon's former headquarters at La Belle Alliance. This signified the end of the battle."

James took a deep breath and finished his wine, then shrugged his shoulders.

"Of course, I don't know everything that went on during those dark days, but I'm sure someone will have read it in full." he grinned. "Being the renowned historian he is, Lord Graham, perhaps?"

Lord Graham roared with laughter.

"As I said, on the night before the battle, the weather was miserable and an uncomfortable time was all we had to look forward to. One chap had an umbrella, which by the way afforded some merriment to our people on the march. We had the idea that if planted against the sloping bank of the hedge, and seating ourselves under it, we could afford ourselves some shelter. The owner of the umbrella invited me to sit on one side of the handle whilst he sat on the other. We lit our cigars and became comfortable.

Wellington never cared much for the way we officers dressed, however he was actually rather startled at the sight of the umbrella and denied us the use of it again saying that it would make us look ridiculous in the eyes of the enemy. For my own part, I thought the French looked somewhat envious."

There was complete silence for a few seconds then Sir Henry stood and proposed a toast. Everyone else in room followed suit.

"What happened to Napoleon after Waterloo, Colonel?" A man asked, breaking the uneasy silence.

"Wellington sent an official despatch to England, describing the battle. It must have arrived here around the twenty-first June, as it was published as a London Gazette Extraordinary on the twenty-second."

"By God sir, I still have a copy," Lord Graham, exclaimed.

"How surprising," Lady Graham said, smiling.

James smiled

"Excuse me James, do you mind if I tell a short heart-warming story?" Lord Graham asked.

"Not at all, please continue." James smiled.

"Please do, Lord Graham." Lady Sarah urged.

Lord Graham coughed and began.

"I do believe that a clergyman has bequeathed five-hundred pounds Stirling, to the bravest Englishman from the battle. The Duke of Welling has been asked to nominate someone and I believe he chose Lieutenant Colonel McDonnell of the Coldstream Guards for his defence of Hougoumont."

James started clapping followed by the rest of the guests. "And well deserved," he said, as the applause died down.

Lord Graham held up his hand. "Ah, that isn't all, though," he said, smiling.

"Colonel McDonnell is going to give half of it to Sergeant Fraser. James has already mentioned him and his heroic actions, getting the wagon of cartridges through the lines to replenish the troops, fighting Hougoumont Chateau."

Everyone in the room, including the footmen, began clapping and cheering.

Lord Graham, rolling the brandy balloon in his hands, looked up at the assembled parties. He took a sip from the glass.

"I apologise if I have bored you. As you know, I am very interested in history, and especially the Napoleon campaign. Waterloo decisively ended twenty-five years of fighting between the European powers and France." Lord Graham regained his seat and winked at his wife. "Was I too boring?" he asked.

"Absolutely not!" she laughed, and then turned to others seated at the table.

"Lord Graham my husband is so besotted with Waterloo that he took me there in May." She glanced around the room, watching the stunned faces. There was much whispering. Lady Sarah started sniggering, setting everyone else off.

"Oh, it wasn't at all as I had imagined though. The grass was not stained with blood and gore and someone had actually removed the bodies. I have seen Hougoumont Colonel Tyler, and how you managed to stay alive, is beyond my comprehension. The cannonade had all but demolished the building."

James looked at her and winked. She blushed and started fanning herself with a highly decorated fan.

"Oh well done, Lady Graham." Sarah laughed and clapped her hands.

Lady Graham sipped her wine and continued. "I have stood on the ridge, where once our dear Sir Arthur had commanded the battle. I have seen the knolls where the bodies of the English and the bodies of the Germans lie. There is no knoll for the French, which is very sad. It is actually a beautiful place with rolling farmlands. I am glad I went."

Lord Graham took her hand and gave it a little squeeze.

James looked over at Isobel. "I too, returned to the battlefield. This would have been on the twentieth I believe. It was just before I re- joined Wellington and the allied forces for the advance on Paris. The sight was terrible, carcasses everywhere. There were heaps of wounded men with mangled limbs, unable to move, and dying from untended wounds or simply dying from hunger."

"Was there no one to tend to them?" Lady Graham asked, shocked, and murmurs resonated around the room.

James shook his head. "The Allies had been obliged to take their surgeons and wagons with them, as Napoleon had yet to be captured."

"So Colonel, why did you go back?" Lady Isobel asked, indignantly.

James looked straight at her. "Someone had to collect George's body. I was not going to leave him there to rot. I brought him home to lie with his beloved Mother."

Isobel looked down at her lap, and complete silence enveloped the room.

"Well, I think we have been well and truly entertained." Lord Henry said, breaking the silence. "We are certainly better informed. Thank you James and thank you too, Lord Graham." He toasted the two men.

It was nearly midnight when the guests began to leave, Tyler amongst them.

"James, you really must come again, it has been a most enjoyable evening," Lady Sarah took his arm as they walked into the hallway.

Isobel, who had been loitering, now stepped forward. She held out her hand and James took hold of it and bowed. "I will see you soon, hopefully," she smiled, but there was no warmth in it.

Chapter 14

Pickit awoke at just after six a.m. In any normal summer, it would have been daylight long before now, but in this peculiar summer, with its peculiar weather, light was struggling to seep through his small window. It would be another hour at least before daylight appeared in its entirety.

He washed in cold water, and then dressed in a warm hessian shirt and black knee length breeches. He found his stockings after rummaging through the old sea chest for a few minutes, together his coat and tall hat. His boots stood by the fireplace. He breakfasted on a crust of stale bread and cheese swilled down with a pint of boiling hot tea laced with a good measure of gin.

He looked around the room with its small window and dirty hearth, and could not help but think of those people who would give everything and anything if they had it, to have a place like this.

Pickit had heard about the Mount Tambora volcano in the Dutch East Indies. It had been erupting since 1812. Sailors coming into the Thames had been full of stories about the volcano, holding court in the eating-houses and taverns that lined the wharves of the river, earning themselves food and drinks enough to feed a small army. They had told that in April of 1815, the mountain had gone off with a loud bang and the ash column had risen to 140,000 feet according to witnesses. It was probably the largest ash explosion since the Ice Age.

The ash and dust in the atmosphere took a while to circulate, and the summer of 1815 was not really affected, but, because of other eruptions happening in the area, it had been cold and wet for a number of years.

This summer had been cold, wet, and miserable. It had snowed near London at Easter, and in May. It had rained on most days since then. Due to incessant bad weather, crops were damaged by rainfall; they did not ripen because of the lack of sunlight. Many crops rotted in the fields before they could be harvested, and more rotted after harvesting because it was so damp. Farm labourers in large numbers, found themselves out of work, which added to the influx of soldiers who had been demobbed after the end of the Napoleonic Wars.

Unemployment rose sharply and the price of basic foodstuffs soared. In addition, many people went hungry, famine threatened and disease and infection rose. Riots occurred all over the country and, in one riot; over one hundred food shops were broken into and ransacked.

Pickit felt lucky. He had a roof over his head, food in his belly and money tucked away in safe places. He had a talent for keeping his head above water, when everyone else was drowning. His sole purpose in life was to survive at all cost. He would make sure he would not starve, and right now, he had to make sure someone else would not starve either.

Almost an hour later, Pickit walked along the quayside looking for the vessel on which Toby awaited transportation. Though not large, Pickit hugged the bundle of food and other items toby would need, tightly to his chest.

A few moments later, he saw the ship taking on supplies for the journey, and Pickit broke into a fast sprint. It took him a further twenty minutes and a large bribe to gain access to his friend.

They stood at the rail, and looked out over the Thames as the waft of sewage hit their nostrils. Even though the breeze should have blown the stench in the opposite direction, the smell clung to their hair, their clothes and seemed to permeate their skin.

"Thanks, lad, for the money, and the other stuff, of course. I will pay ye back fourfold one day," Toby said as he took hold of Pickit's arm.

"Hey, wouldn't ya do the same for me?" Pickit asked.

Toby smiled. "I won't be a prisoner for long. Seven years they say, at the most, and then they let ya loose. I will still be young and hopefully in good health. In seven years, I can learn and I can plan. New Holland, hey? Well, I look on everything as a chance to better meself and I am going to make the most of it, a new country with new opportunities, and I'm gonna grab 'em by the throat."

"Let me know when ya make yer first million and I'll come and collect my debt, plus interest." Both of them laughed.

They saw that visitors were leaving, and they made their way to the queue. Suddenly, Toby grabbed hold of Pickit's arm. "Listen, I got me a sister," he blurted. "I ain't seen her since I got incinerated."

"Incarcerated," Pickit, corrected, laughing.

"Ne'er mind that. You got to find her, tell her where I am and that I am all right. She does not know where I am. Tell her I'll send for her when I get out of this mess."

Pickit frowned, "When did you last see her?"

"Just afore I was arrested."

"What's her name?" Pickit asked.

"Constance. Her name is Constance; she is sixteen and scrubs floors, cleans rooms and waits tables in a hostelry on the Radcliffe Highway. It won't be long before they move her on to other occupations, if they haven't already. That is all I know. Take care of her. Find her Pickit, as I know you will. Do not let her disappear, or she will end up dead in a gutter somewhere. I could not take care of her, but perhaps you might. I will be forever in your debt if you do this for me."

Pickit grabbed his friend and gave him a quick hug. "I promise," he whispered against Toby's ear, and then he was gone.

Toby stood on the deck until they came to take him down below. He wondered if he would ever come back to this, the land of his birth, if he would ever see his sister or Pickit again. He picked up the heavy chains attached to his ankles and wrists, then followed his fellow travelling companions, consisting of convicts, families and his gaolers, down into the bowels of the vessel. It would be many weeks before he saw the light of day again, and mere glimpses at that...if he managed to survive the harsh journey. He did have a better chance than most, thanks to the generosity of his friend.

*Chapter 15*

Pickit knew that it would only be a short brisk walk from the docks to the Radcliffe Highway, and decided to try to find Toby's sister now, rather than go back to the Dials and have to make the arduous journey back, another day. He had a vague idea where the lodging houses and taverns were grouped, but it was not an area he was totally familiar or comfortable with. He heard a clock striking the half hour. It was only ten thirty a.m. He had almost the whole day to find his best friend's sister. Toby had said it was a hostelry, not a lodging house or tavern. How many hostelries were there on the Highway? There could not be that many surely, so it should be an easy task.

After two hours, Pickit was losing hope. No one seemed to have heard of Constance and it was as if she didn't exist. A bowl of slops came cascading down from an open window, and he managed to skip out of the way just in time.

"Oi, watch what you're doin'," he yelled, brushing any stray drops from his jacket.

"Sorry, Mista," came the reply. Pickit looked up and saw a mirror image of Toby but with feminine features and long dark hair. She was about to close the window when Pickit shouted. "Stop, wait up there."

The head poked out again, and she looked down at him. "What now? I missed, didn't I?"

"Do you 'ave a brother?" Pickit asked.

"And who wants to know?" she asked, indignantly.

"Is your brother a lad called Toby?" The sun, as weak as it was, shone straight into Pickit's eyes causing him to shade them with his hand.

"Oh gawd, what's he gone and done now?"

"Can ya come down, me neck's aching."

The window slammed shut and Pickit rubbed the back of his neck.

She was walking fast, almost running, as she came out of the building and, grabbing his hand, she hastily dragged him into a dark alley.

"What's he done now?" she stood with her hands on her hips and she was breathing heavily.

"He tried to kill someone. In self-defence it was," Pickit all but whispered.

The girl stood with her mouth agape, trying to take in what he had just said. She crumbled to the floor,

"Oh gawd, they'll 'ang him," tears started rolling down her cheeks and Pickit knelt before her, taking her hands in his.

"No, no they won't. As I said, it was self-defence; he's got seven years on a penal colony, New Holland it is. He'll be alright; he's tough as ol' boots."

That statement seemed to make her wail even more.

"It's alright," Pickit soothed. "He'll be alright."

"I need to see him," she sobbed.

"Ah well, there might be a problem with that. You see, his ship sailed a couple of hours ago." Pickit kept hold of her hands, afraid that she may strike him at any moment, but she only sobbed, occasionally wiping tears and snot from her face with her apron.

"That's it. I'm done for now," she said as soon as she could get the words out.

"What do you mean?" he asked.

"Toby gave my gaffa a few coins occasionally, so that he wouldn't let the customers have me."

"Have you?" Pickit looked perplexed.

"You know, made sure they kept their filthy hands to themselves."

Pickit nodded, now totally understanding the situation. "I want you to come with me. I promised Toby I would take care of you."

"Oh right! Now you want to take bloody advantage, so who are you anyway?" she attempted to slap him, but he darted out of the way.

"My name's Pickit, I'll leave you to them then."

She calmed down immediately. "No, no don't leave me here," she pleaded.

"How come nobody knew you when I asked about you earlier?" Pickit helped her to her feet.

She looked horrified. "You have been asking about me? We have to go now, before they realise I'm not cleaning the bedrooms," she took his hand and led him further into the passage.

"We can go to Prince's Square from here. Then they'll have a job trying to find us if we keep moving."

"Well, I'll have to follow you; I don't know this area very well."

"Where are we going anyway?" Constance asked.

"I have a friend; well I work for him sometimes. His missus, huge woman she is, with a heart as big as her belly. She will know what to do. I can fend for meself, but…well my place is not exactly a palace. Not a place for a woman."

She grabbed his arm. "Don't leave me, Pickit. I don't want to be alone."

"You won't be. I promised Toby I would take care of you and I will." Pickit smiled at her.

She hesitated. "Well, if Toby told you where to find me, then you must be trustworthy. One wrong move though…" she let the statement hang in the air.

*Chapter 16*

It was early afternoon when they found themselves on the Strand.

"Jack lives on a street just off Drury Lane," Pickit informed her. It was getting chilly, and he sensed that Connie was shivering. He took hold of her hand. "We'll soon be there," he promised.

Within twenty minutes, Pickit was knocking on the door of a well-presented house, tucked away in a small terrace.

The door opened, and Pickit looked down into the grubby face of a small child of indeterminate years.

"Hello, Cyril, is your Ma at home?" Picked asked.

"Yeah, she's in the back yard," the child pointed over his shoulder.

"Lock the door behind us, there's a good lad," Pickit ordered, as he led Constance through the house.

Bessie was just coming through the scullery into the neat little room with its overstuffed couch and wooden settle. A large wooden table surrounded by an assortment of mismatched chairs, was pushed up against a wall. A fire was blazing in the hearth, and three lighted candles complete with candelabra stood on a chest of drawers.

"Well, well. Look what the cat dragged in," she bellowed, as she grabbed Pickit and held him tight against her bosom.

The boy struggled out of her grasp. "Give o'er woman; you'll stifle me to death."

Bessie stood with her hands on her ample hips as she looked Constance over. "And who is this fine looking wench who you have managed to coerce into your miserable little life?"

Pickit grinned. "She's a friend of mine."

Bessie's eyebrows rose up into her hairline. "You ain't got any friends," she laughed.

"Remember Toby Fowler?" Pickit asked.

"Oh aye, I do. Gone off to foreign parts so I heard," she pointed at Constance. "You have a striking resemblance to that young man."

"I'm his sister," Constance stated.

"Aye well, I won't speak ill of him, did us all a good turn when he despatched that thieving, murdering little rat to other parts o' the country." She turned to look at Pickit. "So are you going to tell me what you are both doing here?"

"Ah well, I was hoping Connie could stay here for a while. She can't go back to that dump where I found her, that's for sure."

Bessie turned to Connie, "And what dump was that then?"

Pickit opened his mouth to speak, but Bessie held up her hand to quieten him. "The lass can speak for herself I'm sure."

"The Dog and Bull on the Highway."

Bessie paled. "Radcliffe Highway?"

Connie nodded.

"Well, we'll say no more about that den of iniquity. I'm just surprised that you got out of it with your life intact."

"Toby used to pay them to keep away from her, but now he's gone ... well, she wouldn't have stood much of a chance," Pickit looked down at the floor. He could feel the heat on his cheeks.

"Well, you'll have to sleep in the garret with my three eldest girls. There is only one bed up there, so you'll have to top and tail. I keep asking Jack to get more beds, but I get more sense out of the dog."

Constance looked down at her feet. "But I don't have any money."

"Listen, love, I got eight kids between the ages of two and twelve. A bit of help around here would not go amiss. You can earn your keep. I could surely do with an extra pair o' hands," Bessie looked at Connie with a questioning expression on her face.

Connie smiled broadly, "I think that would be a grand idea."

"There's one thing about my man, he keeps good food on the table, coal in the coal shed, and clothes on our backs. Speaking of which," Bessie fingered the thin material of the girls dress, "We'll have to do something about that," she grumbled.

"Is that all, is that the only dress you got?"

Connie felt her face flush as she looked down to the floor.

"Well, ne'er mind, we'll soon get you sorted," Bessie smiled, kindly.

"Pickit, shift your arse and go home. I think Jack is looking for you. This lass will be safe now. Shows you have some sense in that useless head o' yours. Oh, and don't come calling every five minutes. You want to see each other, you make proper arrangements. Is that clear? I don't need any more kids running amok in my house."

"Oh but we're not...er...we don't...wouldn't...," Pickit stammered, his face reddening.

Bessie laughed. "Not yet you don't, but never say never lad. Now hop it. I have things to do."

Chapter 17

Tyler groaned as he tried to sit up in the bed. There seemed to be a little man with a very big hammer, banging away inside his skull, threatening to smash it. He hadn't realised just how much wine he had drunk the night before, though he vaguely remembered not having to ask for his glass be refilled all evening.

There was a gentle rap on the bedroom door, and Arthur entered. "Good morning Colonel," he said softly. "I have one of Mrs Ash's famous cure-alls, and I would like you to drink it."

"Go away, Arthur, and leave me alone to die."

Arthur took the glass and forced it into Tyler's hand. "You will feel like a new man in a few moments, so drink…please, sir."

"It smells revolting," James groaned, sniffing the contents.

"Hold your nose and throw it down your throat. Trust me, sir."

James did as he had been told. He shuddered violently and grimaced as the liquid hit his stomach. He began heaving and gasping for breath, but within a couple of moments, the spasm subsided.

"God Almighty man, are you trying to kill me?"

Arthur smiled as he took hold of the empty glass. "How do you feel now, sir?"

James looked up at his servant. "Well, er, I suppose better, really. At least, the headache isn't so bad," he gave a huge burp.

Arthur smiled. "And your stomach is settling down nicely too?"

"What the hell is in that stuff?" James asked, swinging his legs out of the bed.

Arthur was opening the curtains. "I have never been able to persuade Mrs Ash to divulge her closely guarded secrets, although I do believe she is passing on some of her recipes to Lizzie."

"Well, just remind me in future not to drink too much, or I will have this to look forward to on the following morning."

Arthur walked towards the slightly opened door. "Oh, and Lady Isobel is waiting for you in the drawing room. I would recommend that you have something to eat before conducting any interviews. Shall I bring something up on a tray?"

James was stunned. He didn't know now, which was worse, Mrs Ash's poison or a meeting with Isobel. He decided he would rather face a dozen glasses of Mrs Ash's lethal brew, than face Isobel on an empty stomach

"Bring me a tray please Arthur, and make my excuses if you would."

Arthur bowed. "I already have, Colonel. The lady thinks you are out taking the morning air."

James smiled. "A gem, Arthur, a real gem, that's what you are."

Thirty minutes later, James felt refreshed. He had eaten a hearty breakfast, washed, shaved and dressed. He looked at himself in the full-length mirror in his dressing room. He was wearing a black tailcoat with a high collar, steel grey trousers and patent leather shoes. Under the coat, he wore a white shirt and cravat, and a silver brocade waistcoat.

He inhaled deeply and walked from the room.

He hesitated for a moment before throwing open the double doors to the drawing room. Isobel was sitting near the fire, holding a cup of tea. As he entered, she placed the china cup and saucer on a mahogany side table and stood. Smiling, she held out her hand.

"I am so sorry to have kept you waiting, please accept my apologies," he took her hand and kissed it.

"No, no, please, Colonel, my fault entirely. I should have made an appointment. Ma-ma would have been horrified, but as I just was passing, I thought that I would pay my respects."

James, still reeling from the heady smell of her exotic perfume, wondered where she could have been going to be 'just passing' his house.

He desperately wanted to sit; his legs were shaking so badly that he wondered why she hadn't noticed.

He indicated the chair, which only a few moments ago, she had vacated.

He took the chair opposite and using a cup, that Arthur had thoughtfully provided, poured himself a cup of tea.

"So, is there any other reason why you wish to see me, other than you "just passing?" he sipped the hot tea so he wouldn't have to look into her dark, mysterious, cruel eyes.

She was dressed in the modern style, a long, straight, loose, cream dress, tied just under her bosom, cream gloves and a bonnet decorated with small lavender flowers. Arthur had obviously removed her coat to the cloakroom.

She put her cup and saucer down on the side table.

"As you know George, that is Colonel Radcliffe and I were, how shall I put it? Close. In fact, we had an understanding."

James looked suitably surprised. "George, of course, didn't always relay his thoughts, actions or intentions to me," he smiled.

"No, I don't suppose for one moment that he did." she relaxed a little. "Yes, we had often talked about marrying when I was of age, but then of course, there never seemed to be time. There was always something happening in the world, and he had to be off and away. Then the Peninsula wars ended, and we thought that at last we could become man and wife. He said we would live in this house and raise many children. We would be the darlings of society. George, the handsome warrior, and me, his dutiful wife."

James coughed and excused himself. "This tea is rather hot," he explained whilst dabbing his lips on a napkin, which had been placed on the table. "Please, do go on."

She smiled sweetly, and then frowned. "Then of course Napoleon escaped and turned my life upside down. All my dreams died in a far distant land, in a hail of canon-fire and sword play." She took a deep breath, and for a moment, James thought she might cry.

She looked at him and James waited. "George told me that he had willed everything he owned, to you, but, as we were now to be married, he would have to change it," she dabbed her eyes with a lace handkerchief, though Tyler hadn't seen any tears so far.

She sat quietly for a few moments, twisting the handkerchief in her lap.

"I found out that I was with child, the day after I heard that George had been killed."

Tyler felt as though he had been hit by the same cannonball that had taken off his friend's head.

"I went to stay with some dear, very discreet friends who live out of town. My parents thought I had gone because I needed the time to grieve, and they were in part, right, but I also needed to have the child without anyone knowing."

Isobel stood and went to the window. "Just before the baby was born, I found out that George had not changed his will. To say this was the worst news is quite an understatement. I was carrying an illegitimate child whose father was dead and had not left us a brass farthing. I was in a state of shock; I just could not comprehend how my world was falling apart."

Tyler's head was swimming, he felt as though he was on the outside looking in, and he could not grab hold of reality. In all the years that they had been friends, George had never even mentioned Isobel, let alone told him of any desires to marry her, and yet, on the many battlefields on which they had found themselves, they had talked of their lives and their plans. Never in all those years, had either one of them, discussed thoughts of marriage.

"You are very quiet, Colonel. Are you now wondering what is going to happen to your cosy little world, now that you know George has an heir?"

Tyler stood and went over to her. "And where is this child now?" He tried to speak calmly, though his whole body was in turmoil.

"Oh, the baby is somewhere safe. I would hate anything to happen to him."

"So it's a boy?"

She smiled. "Of course, the family name has to be carried forward."

James suddenly hated the woman now standing before him, and wanted to stick a knife in her ribs.

"And this child, are you sure it was fathered by George?"

The transformation was instant. Her face reddened with fury. "Fighting dirty now are we, Colonel?" she spat. "Of course he was fathered by George. I'm not in the habit of letting any filth put his hands on me."

She turned and looked out of the window. The sun was fighting a losing battle with the grey, leaden skies.

"So you still haven't told your father?" James tried to keep his voice from rising.

"No, I have not. Though as soon as you have done the decent thing and cancelled all claims to George's fortune, then I will tell them."

"And what if I tell them?" James said.

"Oh, you shouldn't do that, sir; you would make such a fool of yourself, when I deny everything. It could be thought that I spurned your advances, and that you were taking your revenge by sullying my good name. I would then get rid of the boy, and go on with my life. Do you really want to see the child in the workhouse? I do not much care for children Colonel, so I would not really care where he ends up, when he is no longer of any use to me. My father, of course, would cut all ties with you and no doubt brandish your name all over London as a man not to be trusted."

"How can you get rid of your son, like…like an old dress you no longer need?" Tyler felt angrier than he had ever felt, but, more than that, he was utterly disgusted with her.

"The child is a means to an end Colonel, nothing more."

"Get out of my house!" Tyler hissed.

"It may be your house for now Colonel, though not for much longer. I see by your concern, that you will not let anything untoward happen to the boy. I do not think that I will have to wait too long before you do the right thing for your friend's son. Oh, by the way, how did George die?"

"They blew his head off with a cannonball. Now get out!" He grabbed her elbow and hurried her to the door. She tried to struggle out of his grasp, but his hold on her was firm.

"Arthur!" he shouted.

"Sir," Arthur appeared, seemingly from nowhere.

"See Miss Isobel out, will you," he almost threw her out of the room.

*Chapter 18*

Tyler stormed back into the drawing room and slammed the door. He walked over to the window, where he stood trying to calm his temper. A few minutes later, there was a knock on the door, but before James could speak; Arthur walked into the room and closed the doors behind him.

"What is it?" James snapped. He was still standing looking out of the window, his hands clasped behind his back.

"Forgive me, Colonel, but I am aware of a certain tension about your person," Tyler turned to look at his servant, but, before he could speak, Arthur spoke again.

"Colonel Radcliffe was an ardent diarist; actually it was a passion with him."

"Yes, I am aware of that fact, thank you," Tyler said sharply, still trying to calm his temper.

"May I be so bold as to ask you Colonel, have you examined the contents of Master George's trunk?"

James frowned in puzzlement. "Er no, not yet. Why?"

"Then may I suggest that you do so. I think you might find something that will put your mind at rest. All his journals will be there, and as you know, the Colonel recorded every daily event, no matter how insignificant," Arthur opened the door, and as he turned to close it, he winked at James who was standing open-mouthed. Arthur closed the door behind him.

James ran up the wide staircase and threw open his bedroom door. The chest stood at the foot of the bed, where the deliverymen had been told to leave it. He looked around the room and wondered where the keys had been put. He tried the drawers in the small writing table near one of the windows. They weren't there. He then tried the drawers in the bedside tables. They were not there either. He stood with one hand on his hip and the other scratching the back of his head. Just at that moment, Arthur, carrying a tray bearing a cup of tea, entered the room.

"Lunch will be ready in thirty minutes Colonel," He placed the tray on a small occasional table, standing in the centre of the room. Two Regency styled armchairs flanked the table.

"Arthur, just the man I wanted to see," James smiled.

"Colonel, Sir?" Arthur looked puzzled.

"The keys to the chest, do you know where they are?"

"Why yes Colonel. They are in the wall safe. I found them lying on the bed."

James was startled. "Wall safe? I didn't know we had a wall safe."

Arthur walked over to a large painting of Turner's 1813 watercolour "Ivy Bridge", hanging on the wall between the windows. He lifted it down revealing the safe to James.

"Up until today, only Colonel Radcliffe and I knew about this, and the mason who installed it, of course. It will remain a secret with me until the day I expire."

"Ah, but do you know how to open the damn thing?" James asked, peering at the dial.

"Oh yes, sir, Master George imparted that information before he left to go to war. Just in case anything….the numbers would be changed upon his return home."

James rubbed his hands together. "Right Arthur, let's do it!"

A few minutes later, the door was open and James was holding four keys, which he had removed from the safe.

Arthur pointed to the two smaller keys. "Those will open the chest, but I have no idea what the other two are used for. He never did tell me."

James frowned. "Mmm, well, no doubt we will find out in time. Arthur, were you and George very close? He spoke about you of course, and now I find he charged you with a few little secrets."

"I have known Master George since he was born. I was a young footman then, and having him toddling around the house was like a breath of fresh air. When his father died, everyone was devastated; especially Lady Radcliffe, who was very badly affected by the death, and became a recluse. That's when I took it upon myself to make sure that Master George was taken care of, played with and taken for walks in the park. I really enjoyed it, though I have to say that up until that point, I had not really had much to do with children.

"Then Lady Radcliffe died. Oh dear, that was an awful time. George, er Master George was away with his regiment."

"Yes, I remember it well. George was inconsolable," James said, remembering the grief, which his friend had suffered.

"So, whenever he came home, my dear wife and I would try to make him as comfortable as possible. He confided in me and at first, but I tried to discourage it as Master and servant should not socialise. However, he insisted, and he really did not have anyone else apart from yourself, sir, and you could not always be there."

"I wouldn't presume for one moment that you and I could have a relationship that close, but I do appreciate all the help and advice that you have passed on, and I hope that, long may it last."

Arthur bowed his head slightly. "My pleasure Colonel. Master George once told me that he looked on you as his brother, so I will help and guide you, as he would have wished me to. I will leave you now. Would you prefer your lunch on a tray here, or will you grace the dining room?"

James smiled. "Here would be excellent."

Arthur left the room, leaving James to explore the chest.

*Chapter 19*

Tyler found eight volumes of George's diary, covering the years 1808 to half way through 1815, when his writings abruptly stopped.

James would read them all in time, but for now, he was looking for a specific period. He picked up the volumes for the years 1814-1815 and, after making himself comfortable in the armchair; he started reading from the end of November 1814.

The leather-bound books were at least eight inches by ten inches, and three inches thick, and George's writing filled each page.

It was obvious to the reader that there had been a few dinner parties leading up to the First of January 1815 and, a few celebrations in the following weeks. One thing was obvious from the very first few paragraphs: George had made a point of avoiding Isobel Banks and anywhere she usually frequented, as much as he was able.

Naturally, he could not avoid her all of the time, but, when confronted, he would not go anywhere where they would be alone.

One paragraph 'more or less' summed the whole thing up.

"Had dinner at C......'s this evening. I sat next to Sir William Terrence, who is up from Oxford for the festivities. He is a grand chap, delightfully funny, and full of anecdotes and supposedly true, very funny stories. I really take delight in his friendship and company. I find it such a pleasure when there is just the two of us. We get on so well.

Isobel Banks was there, of course. Isn't she always? She is such a nuisance really. Isobel was quite taken with Terence, but it was obvious that he found her annoyingly boring. She would interrupt his conversation to speak to me, probably to get a reaction from him. Of course, he didn't rise to the bait, his attentions being firmly placed at my door. This seemed to enrage her somewhat, and I must admit that I took great delight in watching her striving to keep her emotions in check. Finally, the women left us to our brandy and cigars, although, before leaving, Isobel managed to pass me a note telling me that I should meet her in the garden later. Of course, I didn't go, it was blowing a gale out there and snowing heavily, and I was not going to risk my health for that woman. Naturally, she would scold me, probably in public as usual, but I no longer care. I have no need of her. William being my guest, is now my only concern.

James was confused, and it took a few moments before he understood the implication in his friend's writings. He closed the book when there was a knock on the door. Arthur walked in, pushing a small, silver lunch trolley.

"I have brought a bowl of partridge soup and some cold meats, sir. I thought a small glass of wine now, and perhaps a pot of tea afterwards, Colonel?"

"Well done, Arthur. I hope that your dear wife has provided a slice of her beautiful walnut cake?"

"Oh yes Colonel, she knows now how much you like it," Arthur smiled and turned to leave.

"Arthur, can I ask you something?"

"Of course, Colonel, you can ask anything."

"Have you ever read any of Colonel Radcliffe's journals?"

Arthur looked stunned. "Oh no sir. Colonel George kept always them under lock and key."

"Perhaps in the safe?"

"Definitely not, sir. He always kept them in the trunk, all that is, except the one on which he was working. If he was here at home, it would be locked in his desk drawer," he indicated the desk in the corner, remembering at that moment, that the two spare keys would probably fit the desk drawer, and pointed that fact out to the Colonel.

"And no one else knows about the journals, or what is in them?"

Arthur looked a little uneasy. "No one else knows. However…"

"Yes?" James looked at him.

"I knew of them, sir, though I do not know what they contain."

"But you pointed me in their direction, thinking perhaps there was something in them that might be helpful?"

"Yes sir, I did. I know that Master George was plagued by a certain Lady Isobel, and after what happened earlier today, I am concerned that history that may repeat itself. It crossed my mind that if you read the journals, you would see what kind of person you are dealing with, as I am sure Master George would have written about such a serious matter."

"Did you hear any of that conversation this morning?"

"Not really sir, I could hear raised voices of course, but nothing more. Only when you opened the door, and almost threw out Lady Isobel, did I realise there was something terribly amiss."

James frowned, "Oh dear, was it that obvious?"

"Yes sir, I am afraid it was. Though, may I be very open with you Colonel?"

"Of course, by all means Arthur."

Arthur cleared his throat. "I do wish Master George had done as you did."

James smiled. "So do I Arthur."

"May I speak frankly, Colonel?"

"Why stop now? Please do."

"I hope that you can resolve this. Because of Lady Isobel, Master George never really enjoyed his home. He was terribly afraid that he could never to come here and relax."

"Did Lady Isobel come here often?"

"For some time yes, but they would often argue, no, that isn't strictly true, she would try to goad him, and then Master George would get to the point, where he would tell me, to inform her that he wasn't at home. It wasn't that he was frightened of her; he wanted to avoid any unpleasantness. Anyway, he started spending more time with Mr Terrence or your good self."

"Thank you, Arthur."

"Will that be all, sir?"

"Yes, for now."

Arthur bowed, "Enjoy your meal, sir."

James smiled as the butler left the room.

He continued reading, though nothing seemed to have happened during the first two weeks of January. Then the entry for the 16th of the month drew his full attention.

*I wrote to James a couple of days ago, suggesting we go up to Norfolk for a few weeks. I am bored of London, and Mr Ash and his family are going to be away on much neglected family business, so there is nothing to keep me here.*

*I received James's reply yesterday, saying he would be delighted to join me. This news has really lifted my spirits. I know the house is gone, but mother kept the lodge, thank the Lord. A bit of hunting and fishing is always good for the soul. I may even invite a couple of our unmarried friends, especially Sir William Terence. I have so missed him. He is such jolly company and so very attentive, though I suppose, with the others here, we will have to kerb our humour.*

*We will be meeting up there on the 20th*

"Yes!" James exclaimed loudly. He remembered it well.

For most of the time in Norfolk, the men had taken care of themselves. A Mrs Coulter came up from the village in her little pony and trap, every couple of days, to clean and tidy up after them. She also came bearing eggs, bread and cold meats and any other sundries, which they needed.

George would repay her with some of the game, which they had managed to bag, along with few silver coins.

Most evenings were spent, engrossed in games of backgammon, chess or cards. These were usually bawdy affairs due to the copious amounts of wine and spirits consumed. It was only now, that he remembered that when everyone else retired for the night, George and young Master Terrence would often stay up.

One morning, on his way down to breakfast, James had seen Terrence leaving George's room, but thought nothing of it. "Just making sure George is awake." Terrence explained. "A good day for hunting. Will you be joining us, James?"

Whilst reflecting, James could not remember the date that they had returned to London, but he remembered why. Napoleon had escaped from Elba and was now forming an army. James leafed through the journal. The date Napoleon had escaped was March 1st 1815. On the 19th March, he had resumed his position of Emperor of France.

According to George's Journal, Mrs Coulter had brought a messenger up to the Lodge. He bore the news that both he and George had been recalled to their regiment.

George left for his home in London as did the others, and James returned to his old lodging house to collect his trunk and pay his landlady his past dues.

Sometime later, James along with his friend George had arrived on the continent. Sir Arthur Wesley, the Duke of Wellington, was gathering the forces, for what hopefully be would be the final battle against Napoleon.

James closed the book. He now knew that Isobel's story was a total fabrication, as from the end of January, George had not had any contact with her at all, for he had been in Norfolk. George's home visit was brief. He stayed only for a few nights, and apart from the servants, according to the diary, he had met no one.

Throughout the time spent in Norfolk, James had noticed that Sir William and his friend George had some kind of bond, a closeness not shared with others, and one to which James was not privy. He now considered this. Tyler walked over to the fireplace and tugged on the bell-pull.

Tyler was just finishing the last of his lunch, when Arthur entered the room.

"You rang, sir?"

"I did, Arthur. No, leave that a moment," he put out his hand as Arthur was about to take the trolley away.

"Sir?" Arthur looked puzzled.

"I just need you to confirm something for me; though it was some time ago, and you may not remember."

"I will do my best, sir."

"Cast your mind back. Between the first of January and the last week of that month, did Colonel Radcliffe at any time see Lady Isobel?"

"That was in January 1815, sir?"

James nodded.

"Oh, I would doubt it. Sir Henry and Lady Sarah would be extremely busy at that time. They usually are, and Lady Isobel would not be allowed to shirk her duties. As you know sir, they do entertain a great deal and, especially at that time of year. They would be returning dinner invitations and so on. Sir Henry has a lot of business associates and they do entertain rather much."

"Did Master George attend any of these functions?"

Arthur thought for a moment. "No, I really don't think he did."

"Do you know whether he would have attended any functions where Lady Isobel might have been present?"

Arthur frowned. "I believe the Colonel attended a few Regimental dinners, but I doubt very much that Lady Isobel would have been invited. He attended those functions with either yourself, or if you were unavailable, he would take Sir William as his guest."

"Quite right, Arthur. I attended a few of those same functions and no, that lady wasn't there."

"Is that all, sir?"

James smiled. "Yes. Thank you, Arthur."

Arthur bowed slightly and turned to leave the room.

As he reached the door, he turned. "Excuse me, sir."

"Yes?"

"I believe it was about the end of the second week in December. Lady Isobel called, and appeared to be in a rather agitated state. Master George took her into the drawing room, and although the doors were closed, I could hear the most furious shouting. It was mainly Lady Isobel's voice."

"And could you hear what was being said?"

"Not really, sir. I did hear her say that he would rue the day that he turned his back on her. Other than that, I really couldn't say." James paced the room, his hands behind his back.

Arthur continued, "After a short while, she left the house. Master George told her not to return."

"Really?" James had stopped his pacing.

"Well…Master George was rather angry, though he really tried to hide it. He called all the servants together. There were more of us in those days, and he told us never to allow her over the threshold again."

"And did she call again?"

"Oh yes, but I did as I was instructed. I always told her that the master was away from home, and after about the fourth or it may have been the fifth time, she never came again. Well not until today, sir."

"So am I right in thinking that George and Isobel probably hadn't seen each other since before Christmas of 1814?"

"Oh I couldn't be certain sir, but I think it highly likely." Arthur turned to leave the room then hesitated. James looked at him, quizzically.

"I do hope she isn't going to make more trouble, Colonel."

James laughed. "I have handled a lot of mean tempered fillies in my time, Arthur. I will not let that one get the better of me."

Arthur smiled, "No, sir, I believe you won't."

James spent many hours over the next few days, reading his friend's journals. Sometimes, he felt as though he was prying deeply into George's mind. However, he was doing this, not just for himself, but also for George, as there was no knowing when Isobel Banks would be back with more lies. If this were going to be the case, he would be prepared. He would know more about George than anyone else could possibly know. He also wanted to talk to Sir William Terrence, discretely of course, to form some idea of the man with whom George was so infatuated.

James knew Terrence of course, and found him to be handsome, witty and charming and always thought him to be a ladies' man. William, though, obviously liked beautiful people of both genders.

Colonel James Robert Tyler grinned. He had just declared war on Isobel Banks, and she would soon see that he was not quite as charming as Colonel George Radcliffe was. He was going to enjoy this. He pulled the cord, and within moments, Arthur appeared.

"You rang, sir?"

"Yes Arthur. I think I may have found something that might just make Lady Isobel leave us all alone."

Arthur's face brightened. "Is that so sir?"

James nodded. "I need to contact Sir William Terrence. Do you know where I can find him?"

"No, but I am sure Sir George would have put the details in his address book. You will, in all probability, find that in the trunk, or in his desk drawer."

*Chapter 20*

Pickit awoke with a start: someone was hammering on the door. He sat up, and as he tried to get off the pallet that was his bed. His legs became tangled in the bed coverings and he ended up in a heap on the cold floor. He cursed as he bumped his shin. He threw on his clothes, such as they were, and went to the door.

The hammering on the door became more urgent.

"Hold it will you? I'm coming. Who is it?" he shouted. There was silence.

"What do you want?" he shouted again.

"Pickit, let me in, it's Colonel Tyler."

The boy fumbled with the lock and key, and the door creaked open.

"Crikey sir, you gave me a fright, so you did," Pickit opened the door wider, and the Colonel strode in.

Pickit, wearing just a pair of pantaloons and an old shirt, threw some wood and coals onto the embers of the fire, and by the time the kettle had been filled and placed on the chimney hook, the fire was burning well.

Tyler stood with his back to the fire, relishing the warmth against his legs. Pickit busied himself getting dressed.

"I have tea and I have gin, but not a lot else," the boy explained.

"Both would be good," Tyler replied.

"I didn't think ya would be able to find this place again, and how do ya know I was down here anyway?"

"I've got a good memory, and I saw a glimmer of light through that little window."

"Well, how'd ya get in? The door is kept locked."

The Colonel laughed. "You are not the only one who knows how to pick a lock. I learnt many skills in the Army, and not all of them legal."

It was Pickit's turn to laugh, as he now handed the steaming mug to James. They sat side by side on crates in front of the fire.

"This is good," said James, pointing to the mug of tea, which contained more than a generous helping of gin.

"Oh aye, so it is. Mister Scrimms, that's me gaffer, he gets it for me."

"Then perhaps you'll ask him to get me some, sometime."

"Aye, I will," the boy grinned.

There was silence for a few minutes whilst they sipped the hot tea and gin.

"So, what brings ya here then? I'm sure it isn't a social call. Toffs don't usually darken my doorstep."

James shuffled on the wooden crate. "I would like you to do something for me, for which you will be handsomely rewarded."

"So, it ain't legal then?" Pickit asked.

"What makes you think that?" Tyler asked.

"If it were legal, you wouldn't be payin' me and you'd be asking someone else to do it, or... you might even do it yourself."

The Colonel laughed and nodded. "Good point, but you're wrong. I will not be asking you to do anything illegal. As I have already said, you will be paid and you will have some new clothes. Nothing too fancy mind. Are you game lad?"

"Well, I dunno. I'm a bit busy," Pickit frowned.

"Doing what, may I ask?" James face darkened, and Pickit saw something he wasn't too sure about, and didn't really want to find out.

"Well, nothin' that won't keep. Alright, so what is it, then?"

Tyler stood. "I'll let you know in due course," he handed a wad of notes to the boy.

"Buy yourself some good clothes, including boots, and have something done with that mop which is sticking to the top of your head. One more thing, do not wear anything, which you have newly purchased until I tell you. We don't want to draw a crowd, keep it safely out of sight."

Pickit nodded. "You can rely on me Colonel, sir."

"I hope so lad, I certainly hope so. Do this job well and If all goes to plan, you might find yourself wealthier than you ever dreamed possible," James opened the door and let himself out.

Chapter 21

Pickit sat at the makeshift table and looked, at the money that James had left. He pondered the conversation. It had really stunned him, knowing that the Colonel could walk into his life without any further ado. He would change the lock on the outer door and tell Scrimms that he was not too happy with the present security. Scrimms would respect his judgement and would probably even pay for the new lock.

He dressed and let himself out of the room. Within a little while, he was standing outside Jack Scrimms's house. Connie opened the door.

"What are you doing here at this time of the morning?"

Pickit grinned. "I couldn't live for another moment without casting my eyes over your loveliness."

"Who is it?" Bessie called from the depths of the house.

Pickit put his finger to his lips.

"No one important, Misses Bessie," Connie answered, stepping out and closing the door behind her.

Pickit grinned. "Can you get away?"

Connie looked back. "Not now, but perhaps later."

The door had swung open and Bessie was standing there. "Aye, and that'll be only if you finish your work girl. Now get on. What do you want apart from the obvious?" She looked at Pickit.

"Actually, I'm looking for Mister Scrimms. Is he in?"

"You'll probably find him at the inn on King Street. That's where he usually hides his miserable body."

"Thanks, missus. I'll try there then."

As Pickit turned to leave, he found himself face to face with two Bow Street runners. The boy stumbled back.

"Now then, lad, what you up to then? Why are you botherin' these ladies?"

Pickit felt his face flush red, but before he could answer, Bessie pushed her huge bulk through the door and stood with her hands on her ample hips.

"He ain't botherin' anybody. He works fer me husband, and what's it got to do with you anyway?"

The two men stepped back, startled. "Aye well, we were just checking.' Don't want any trouble," they looked at each other, then back at the amazon standing before them.

"Well, take yer concerns somewhere else then," They flinched as Bessie held Pickit's shoulder and dragged him into the house. She slammed the door shut and the frame shook. "Botherin' god-fearin' folks, whatever next? Nosey bloody parkers!" she shouted.

Pickit looked at Connie and grinned.

"Ya can wipe that idiot look off yer face. I've a good mind to take a stick to ya, bringing the law to me own doorstep."

"Me!" Pickit asked, shocked. "I didn't bring 'em did I Connie?"

"Don't get her mixed up in your worthless life. You are gettin' as bad as my husband."

"Aw, come on, Bessie, I ain't that bad," Pickit moaned.

"Go and look, see that they've gone," Bessie told Connie. "Trouble being, we live too near that lot, Bow Street being just around the corner. I'm going to ask Jack to move us away from here."

The girl opened the door a crack, and then leaned out to glance up and down the alley. "They've gone," she announced.

"Right. Now you can clear off as well then," Bessie said. "See him out then Connie, and don't be long," she winked at the girl.

The boy had walked only a few yards when the Runners pounced on him. "Gotcha!"

Pickit tried to squirm out of the man's grasp, but to no avail. "What ya doin'? Leave me alone. I ain't done anything."

"We'll see about that." The two men dragged him along the alley and out onto the street.

Connie was standing on the doorstep whilst all this was going on, and she now ran back into the house, calling for Bessie.

"Good God, girl, whatever is the matter?"

Connie was crying. "They've taken him," she cried.

"Who have? Not those Runners?" Bessie asked, angrily.

"Yes, they've carted him off. What are we going to do? He ain't done anything'."

"Well I dunno about that. P'raps they know somethin' we don't," Bessie said, doubtfully.

Connie was angry now." Well if he has, then Jack's at the bottom of it!"

Bessie looked at the girl as if she was going to hit her. Suddenly, she relaxed. "Aye, you could be right." The woman grabbed her shawl. "Take care of the babies."

"Where are you going?" Connie asked, fearfully.

"First, I'm going to find Jack, good-for-nothing that he is. He'll sort it. If I can't find 'im, then I'll think of something else," With that Bessie hurried from the house.

Pickit sat on the bench in the narrow, dark corridor, nursing his black eye. A chain was padlocked to his leg with the other end attached to the wall behind him. He was thoroughly miserable and seethed angrily. The two men had badgered and banged him about, and had taken the money, which Tyler had given him for new clothes. He looked at the sleeve of his coat, now torn and ragged, as he sat waiting to be questioned.

A door banged open somewhere, and he could hear raised voices. Pickit recognized the dulcet tones of Jack and Bessie Scrimms. He grinned, as he knew that whoever was on the end of their tongue-lashing, would have those voices ringing in his ears for a month. He stood up and tried to peer around the corner of the dividing wall, which separated this part of the building from the main office.

Suddenly, one of his captors marched into the corridor. He batted the side of Pickit's head with the flat of his hand, and the boy sat down on the bench with a thump. His jailor unlocked the chain from Pickit's ankle, and grabbed his arm and marched him through to a small office. Pickit's feet barely touched the floor.

The office probably wasn't small at all, but seemed to be because of the imposing figures of Bessie and Jack.

"Unhand him you thug!" Bessie said, roughly pulling the Runner away from Pickit. She pulled the boy to her ample bosom and stroked his thick, dark hair protectively. Pickit struggled to breathe.

The Runner tried to grab him, but then saw the look on Bessie's face, and put his hands down by his side.

"Right, so what is he supposed to have done?" Jack demanded.

The man, who had unchained the lad, now spoke. "He was seen early this morning leaving a business premises. He was counting a load of money that he had taken from his pocket. He was followed, and he was then seen knocking on the door of a house just off Duke Street. When the door opened, a young female spoke to him, and we got the impression that he was being a pest. We had words with him and then left. A short time later he was apprehended and searched, and was found to be carrying a total of..." he hesitated and looked down at a sheet of paper on the desk," ten pounds sixteen shillings. When questioned he refused to say where this money had come from."

By this time, Jacks face was purple, and Pickit thought that he might burst a blood vessel. He then watched open-mouthed, as Scrimms grabbed the Runner by his collar and pinned him up against the wall. The Runner was tall, probably six feet, but Jack towered over him.

"That money you thieved off an innocent little lad is payment for some goods which I had purchased yesterday at the docks. He was on his way to pay the debt. This lad that you have beaten black and blue, and kept a prisoner, is in my employ. You have not only robbed him and imprisoned him, but by your stupidity, have kept me and him from our employment and my dearest wife here from our dear little children."

Pickit had never seen this side of Jack Scrimms and he watched horrified, as the runner struggled for breath. Suddenly, Jack let go, and the man slid to the floor. The two other Runners in the room had now paled, fearful that the giant standing before them might have a go at them.

Jack straightened his tailcoat and adjusted his hat. "Right, I'll take my money and leave you gents to your own business. Fifteen pounds, if you please," he held out is hand.

The man behind the desk frowned. "It was only ten pounds and..." he closed his mouth when he caught the look on Jack's face. Jack smiled sweetly when the man rummaged through a box and produced fifteen pounds.

"For the inconvenience, like," Jack announced, pocketing the money.

*Chapter 22*

Pickit mopped up the gravy in the bowl with the last of the bread. He glanced over at Bessie and Jack, also tucking into the simple fare. None of them had eaten since early morning, and all three were famished. Jack had hauled them into his favourite eating-house on the Strand, and using some of the money recovered from the Bow Street office, had treated them all to a hearty lunch, swilled down with copious amounts of tea, beer and gin. He had handed the rest of the money to Pickit, who had squirreled it away inside his jacket.

Jack belched loudly and Bessie, sitting next to him, dug him in the ribs with her elbow. "It's like living with a pig," she grumbled.

"Shouldn't you be at home with the young 'uns?" He rubbed his side where her elbow had probably left a large bruise.

Bessie smiled. "Begrudge me an afternoon out with me husband do you? There was a time when I couldn't get rid o' you. Always 'angin' around you were. A right pest."

"Aye well, I got things to do, so you had better be off,"

Bessie winked at Pickit, who was sitting opposite. "You are not getting rid o' me that easy. Connie's taking care o' the babies. So there's no hurry now is there? Pour me some more tea will yer, lad, and put a drop o' that gin in it. Just to warm me. We could go to that new theatre; I've been told there's somethin' called a matinee on."

Jack grimaced. "I ain't got time for all that, Bessie love, I got meetin's and then got to collect some money owed to me."

Bessie groaned. "You always used to make time for me, but now I'm tied down with a crowd o' kids, you're not interested unless you want more babies, that is."

Jack's face reddened. "We'll go next week. I promise," he squeezed her arm lightly.

"I'll be off then. I might be late, so don't wait up."

"If I'm in bed when you get back, don't you dare wake me, I have to be up at the crack of dawn."

"No love, I'll probably fall asleep by the fire."

Bessie glared at him. "Yes, like you usually do. I sometimes wonder how we ever got so many kids."

Pickit sniggered behind his hand.

"Wot you laughin' at?" Jack, with a face like thunder, leant across the table.

Pickit leant backwards and felt the heat rise up from his neck and colour his face. "Nothin' governor," he mumbled.

"Right, better not, is all I can say," Jack touched his wife's shoulder, then walked out of the eating-house.

"Don't be too late," Bessie called after him. Her husband waved without looking back.

"I haven't thanked you properly," Pickit said.

"Think nothin' of it lad, couldn't have that lot locking you up, now could we? What would Jack do without you, anyway?" Bessie took a sip of her tea. "I keep tellin' him that he should get rid of that Barley feller and set you on. Barley gives me the creeps, he does."

"He's alright to me," Pickit defended.

"You ain't a woman. You haven't got curvy bits and a backside he likes to slap. One o' these days I'm going to slap him so hard he'll wake up in the middle of next week."

"He slapped you? Cor, he's a braver man than I gave him credit for," Pickit laughed.

"Aye, well, brave men don't live long in my book. Take those brave soldiers at Waterloo, and other places. Most of 'em didn't come home, did they? Died 'cos they were brave enough to go up against Bonaparte. They should have given that Barley feller the King's shilling. Seen how brave he was then. Umph!"

Pickit smiled. "I know somebody who was at Waterloo."

"Oh aye?" Bessie's eyebrows rose.

"Not a friend as such, he's just an acquaintance really," Pickit explained.

"Officer was he?" Bessie asked

"Oh yes, a Colonel."

Bessie struggled to her feet. "Nothing' like hobnobbing with gentry. If you keep on his good side lad, you won't come to any harm. Anyway, time I was off."

Pickit also stood. "I'll walk you back, then."

*Chapter 23*

Sir William was agitated and paced the room. "Are you intending to blackmail me, sir? Because, if you are, then you may as well forget that idea."

James smiled. "My dear chap, what do you take me for? I am not here for money. All I need to know is, did you and George have a relationship deeper and more meaningful than just friendship?"

"Yes, no, it wasn't like that. I like men but not in the way, you think. And if it isn't money you're after, then why do you need to know?" William Terrence continued to pace the room, clearly still agitated. "I am betrothed to a woman of high standing. If this should become public knowledge, people will get the wrong idea, you know what people are like, and my reputation will be ruined."

James stood and guided Terrence to a chair. "I know, so please do not fear me William: I am your friend. Whatever goes on in this room is entirely between us. I am doing this for George, as there is someone who is about to blacken his name."

Terrence stood, a look of horror crossing his face. "We were not lovers! Good lord Man, what are you thinking? "

James shook his head. "Then I do not understand."

"We were close, and yes, we liked each other, George was probably fonder of me than I of him, but it was nothing more than a deep friendship." Terrence explained. "I really do like the ladies."

James took a deep breath and proceeded to tell the whole story, of how Isobel Banks was trying to blackmail him, with a cock and bull tale of a relationship between herself and George.

"What?" Terrence stormed. "He detested the woman, and I was not over fond of her myself." Terrence was now staring out of the window, his hands clasped tightly behind his back. "So, what exactly does she have to gain from that? She must have known what George thought of her."

James frowned. "She's after my house, my money and anything else, that had George willed to me."

William looked out of the window at the well-manicured lawn. "Well, she won't succeed in that little venture. I am sure there is nothing she can hold over you. Now, if it was I, well, that doesn't bear thinking about."

James shook his head. "She claims to have a child fathered by George."

Terrence laughed. "Now, I doubt very much." Laughing, he turned to look at Tyler. "Was she serious?"

James nodded, "Oh yes, she was serious alright."

"Fair enough, James, I'll tell you what you want to know. I am very protective of George, and it seems that you are too. Yes, we were close, and had been since school. It began, when I came upon him being badly beaten by a few older boys, in an empty classroom. I, being a little older and practiced in boxing, soon despatched the thugs. George, however, had been quite severely injured; they had kicked him in the groin area repeatedly and viciously. He was absent from school for many months, and by the time he returned, the perpetrators had been expelled, one had actually been flogged."

"Why had they done that?" James asked.

Terrence offered James a cigar, which James declined. "I have my own thoughts, but I really don't know for sure. He was of course, exceptionally good looking. He was tall, had blond hair, blue eyes and had a beautiful smile. The girls would swoon if he so much as looked their way. I would imagine this caused a rather a vast amount of jealousy."

James shook his head. "And I never knew."

William nodded. "Although I was older, we remained friends at school, and more so thereafter. We did like to socialise occasionally, as you know, but, once he was in the Army, we had little chance of getting together. When we did go out, I had a wandering eye, but George didn't. You see, he confided to me that the beating had left him disfigured and impotent. He couldn't make love with anyone, a fact he found terribly humiliating and awfully embarrassing. Our secret made our relationship more, well personal, if you get my meaning. I knew things that no one else did. However, nothing physical ever took place, not with anyone. It just wasn't possible, George made that perfectly clear. It always worried him that he couldn't pass on the family titles. He loved women, and would often become involved in a few scrapes, but it never went further than a kiss. He would always find some excuse to extricate himself from a relationship before it became serious. "

James's jaw dropped. "Well I never."

"And nor did he," Terrence smiled.

James burst out laughing and then frowned. "So, why didn't he leave everything to you?"

"Ah, well you see, my dear chap, I am already wealthy. My Grandfather left a huge pot, and my father, when he passes, will leave it all to me. I have no siblings, and I have no cousins either. I am already wealthy beyond words, and I am likely to be more so, in time. You, on the other hand, my dear sir, were not. I knew that George was fond of you. His saviour, he would often say, so he left everything to you as I had advised. I was also one of the three witnesses to the will, and I can say, with hand on heart, that no one deserved it more than you, James."

Terrence sat in a highly decorated, winged back chair. "Now what are we going to do about that awful woman?" he said, almost to himself. "We can't let her go around telling untruths, sullying the good name of Colonel Radcliffe."

"First of all, I would like to find out whether there is a child, and if so, where she is hiding this offspring" James replied.

"Quite right James," William smiled.

Just then, the door opened and a tall, well-dressed gentleman entered. "Ah, there you are, William."

"Papa, I would like you to meet Colonel James Tyler, an acquaintance of mine."

The older man shook James's hand vigorously. "Dammed pleased to meet you sir, I have heard so much about you."

James bowed. "Thank you, sir," he could think of nothing else to say to this man, who was a highly decorated Brigadier with many years of experience in the Napoleonic wars, and was now in government.

"William, I just wanted to let you know that I will be busy for the rest of the day, and will probably dine, and then spend the night at my club. Will you see to your own needs?"

"Yes of course Papa, but don't work too hard, you know what the doctor told you."

Brigadier Terrence grinned at James. "Worse than any wife you know Colonel. Will you be staying for dinner, if so I will inform cook."

Before Tyler could reply, William held his shoulder. "Please do, James. I am desperate for some congenial company."

A few minutes later, the two men were alone once more.

"Now, as you were saying, do you know for certain that the child is a boy?" William asked.

"So she says, but how true it is, I do not know," James replied. "I only know, what that spiteful woman has told me."

Terrence stoked the fire and put on another log. Sparks spluttered out, dying before hitting the Persian carpet.

Sir William stroked his chin. "We will have to hire someone to follow her. I have heard of people that do that for a living."

"What do you mean by 'we'?" James queried.

"Of course, I will not allow you to go through this alone James. After all, George was my friend too."

James smiled. "Thank you, William. I appreciate it and accept your offer. We won't have to employ anyone though, as I know the perfect chap to do the job. In fact, I have already told him that I may need his services."

"Do I know this person?" Terrence asked, re-lighting his cigar.

"Oh, I bloody well hope not, or I shall want to know why you were walking the highways and byways of St Giles, and the slums of this wonderful parish," James doubled up with laughter.

Terrence blushed, and then looked a trifle confused. "So, Colonel, why were you tramping the highways and byways of this un-salubrious area?"

James grinned. "Touché. Long story, but let's just say that the lad in question saved my skin one dark night. He is ambitious, and wants to better himself. I think we can trust him implicitly," James explained.

William nodded. "Can he keep his mouth shut?"

James nodded. "Don't worry. All I want him to do is follow that darn woman. We have to know about that child, more importantly, who his real father is."

William shook Tyler's hand. "We will, James. I am sure we will. So tell me about the boy. You say he has ambitions?"

"I would say the lad is about seventeen or eighteen years old," Tyler replied. "No family whatsoever, he was found on the steps of some old gin palace, when only a couple of hours old. He's been fending for himself for about six years, and not making a bad job of it, either. You should see the squalor some people live in. This lad lives in a small room that I wouldn't keep a dog in. It's situated in a warehouse teeming with rats and as cold as anything I have ever experienced. He works on a casual basis, for some chap who earns his living by smuggling, and any other illegal activity you could bring to mind. The boy strikes me as being intelligent, articulate and shrewd."

"It seems to me, James, that you are the shrewd one. Set the lad to his task forthwith. Let me know if you need anything, I will help all I can."

*Chapter 24*

It was dark when Pickit returned to the warehouse. The smell, which emanated from doorways and open windows as he had made his way along the alleyways, was a mixture of soot, smoke, cooking, rotting food, faeces and rotting vegetation. It didn't bother him; he was used to it and in a few moments, he would be safely inside the warehouse, drinking from the jug of gin which he had tucked inside his ragged coat.

As he turned the corner of the building to unlock the door, a voice startled him, and he nearly dropped the jug.

"Hello Pickit. Just returning from another day of arduous but rewarding labour, are you?"

"Blimey Colonel, you nearly gave me heart failure, so you did."

"What ill-gotten gains are you hiding under your coat?" Tyler asked, pointing to the bulge under the thin material.

"Me supper, that's all," Pickit frowned.

"And are you inviting me to this wonderful feast of yours then? Seeing as I probably paid for it," Tyler tried to muffle his laughter.

"Yeah why not, I could do wi' a bit o' company," Pickit grinned. They entered the dark warehouse, and the boy locked the door behind, them before lighting a lantern and leading the way up the narrow stairway.

James had brought his own bottle of liquor, a fine malt whisky of which he was particularly fond. It was certainly easier on his digestive tract than the lethal brew, which Pickit had supplied.

Pickit made a fire, and both of them sat on the wooden crates, warming themselves.

"I don't know what the weather is supposed to be doing, but if it's this cold in August, what's winter going to be like?" James said, trying to stop his teeth from chattering. He put the whisky bottle to his lip, and swallowed a large mouthful of the contents.

"You're just not used to it," Pickit laughed.

"Aye lad, you're probably right," James said and belched loudly.

"So what brings ya to my door this time?" Pickit asked, poking the fire and adding a few cobbles of coal, which he had purchased sometime before.

"Ah well, I told you that I needed you to do something for me?"

Pickit nodded. "I got the clothes like you said. Nothin' gaudy, but good stuff."

"Good," Tyler smiled and rubbed his hands together. "I want you to follow someone. I'm not much bothered about the general, everyday excursions this person may make, but I do want to know whether she goes anywhere near a house, where a small child could reside. The child would be about a year old. I want to know whether she fusses over it."

"Like a mother would, you mean?" the boy asked.

"Precisely." James smiled. "It's nice to know that I can rely on you to be quick on the uptake."

"Is it hers then?" Pickit frowned.

"I believe so, though I have yet to prove it," James replied.

"So what does this baby look like?" Pickit asked.

"Ah well, there lies a problem, I have no idea."

Pickit patted the Colonel on the arm. "Don't fret, it won't matter none."

James gave Pickit a piece of paper. "This is the address where she lives."

Pickit shook his head.

"Now what's wrong?" James sat up straight and glared at the boy.

"I can't read," Pickit looked down at the floor.

"Oh!" James said surprised at himself that he hadn't given any thought to the idea that the lad couldn't read or write.

"Never mind, I can tell you the address, and better than that, I'll take you there. Come on, drink up and put something warm on. I don't need your death on my conscience."


It was some time later when they found themselves walking along Piccadilly and onwards towards Berkley Square. Pickit suddenly stopped.

"What's wrong?" James asked. The collar of his coat was pulled up around his ears, against the cold night air, and his breath came, in what seemed to be, small puffs of steam.

"I've been here before," Pickit announced, his was voice muffled by the makeshift scarf, which was tied around the lower part of his face. A woolly cap was pulled down on his head to meet the scarf, so that only his eyes were visible.

"Oh yes, to return a wallet, I believe." James sensed Pickit squirm, inside his bulky clothing.

"Well, at least you have it back," Pickit mumbled.

James looked at him, and nodded, he pointed to the house. "She lives there," he announced. "She's young, early twenties with very dark hair. She is slender of figure and walks with her head held high. She looks very much like her mother, but mama is a little more portly. I'm telling you this so that you will know the difference between them. I want her followed every day, until you see her with that child, and at the house in which it lives. I then want you to come back to me with all the details, and then take me if I so wish."

"Name?" Pickit mumbled.

"What? Oh, yes. Isobel Banks. Lady Isobel Banks."

Pickit shuffled his feet, trying to prevent the cold from penetrating the thin soles of his shoes. "Is it his wife then, or daughter, you know the Banks chap?" James nodded. "Daughter."

"Am I allowed to ask why?" Pickit hugged himself, trying to keep warm.

James frowned. "No, the less you know, the better. I will probably tell you later. If you are challenged at all, you will not mention my name, is that clear?"

Pickit nodded. "No need to fear anything, sir, I know when to keep my mouth shut."

"Yes, well, that is just what I had hoped. You will be well paid for your trouble," James turned and looked the lad in the eye. "Very well paid, my friend." James then explained to Pickit where he lived but told Pickit clearly, never to present himself there dressed in his usual rags.

"Take care with your appearance; you do not want to draw attention to yourself or to me, do you understand?"

The boy nodded vigorously.

Pickit felt his heart swell. He had been called friend, and nothing on earth would make him fail in this mission. He walked home with a spring in his step. He felt good, and for the first time in what seemed years, he felt wanted, needed even. It gave him a good feeling and he felt less lonely.

*Chapter 25*


All through what remained of the month of August, and the first week of September, nothing was heard from Pickit. William mentioned that perhaps the lad had been caught dealing in some illegal activity, and was now incarcerated, unable to carry out his duty.

James shook his head. "I would have heard something. The boy has ways and means of communicating, no matter what. We have to be patient. I know it is difficult William, but I trust the lad, if there was anything to report, he would be here as fast as his legs could carry him."

Then, early afternoon on Friday 6th September, there was a loud hammering on Tyler's front door. Arthur arrived in the hallway just ahead of James.

"Someone is in a desperate hurry, wouldn't you say, Colonel?"

"It's alright, Arthur, I will get this. I am expecting someone," James waited until Arthur was making his way down the back stairs, before opening the door.

"Wake the neighbourhood, why don't you?" James whispered, dragging the youth into the house. "Where have you been?" he asked, opening the door to the library and shoving the boy through it.

Pickit waited until James had closed the double doors, before explaining. He removed his hat and scarf, and sat in the chair by the fire, warming his hands.

"Well?" James demanded.

"I ain't been avoiding you, you know. It's just taken me this long to find out what you need to know. These things take time." He stood up, lifted the tail of his coat, and warmed his backside by the fire.

"Just get on with it, lad," James said impatiently.

"Every day I followed that woman, and I was on the verge of giving up, I can tell you. Freezing out there, it was. All she seemed to do was shop, or walk in the park with her friends. Sometimes she would be collected in a carriage, and she would be away for some time. There wasn't any way I could follow her then." Pickit rubbed his hands. "Any chance of something to eat?" He looked expectantly at Tyler. "I'm famished, I ain't eaten all day."

"I'll see to that in a moment. Now what have you discovered?" James was beginning to snap. He tried to calm himself.

Pickit sat down again. "Right. Well, today I took up my usual position by that massive oak tree which is not far from the house. I expected a long wait. During the times I had been keeping an eye on her, she had usually left home about eleven o'clock. Today she was a good bit earlier. She also left in a different direction, which puzzled me somewhat, as I didn't have any hiding places planned. Anyway, it didn't matter, as she didn't turn around once. That is, not until she came to a particular house on a street near the corner of Piccadilly and Hyde Park. I had kept myself at a good distance and hidden slightly by a sycamore tree, so she didn't spot me when she turned around."

Pickit blew into his hands and then rubbed them together.

"Before she had even opened the gate, the door of the house opened, and a big fat woman came out holding a small child. She put him down and he

136

toddled down the path towards the woman. She picked him up and kissed his face. Then...You will like this bit, Colonel. A man appeared who rushed down the path, took the woman and the child in his arms, and kissed them both. They then went into the house."

Tyler grinned like an idiot. "I take it that you can find this house again?" he asked.

"Of course!" the boy answered indignantly. "Anyway, I hung around for a couple of hours, and glad that I did. It was about two hours later when she came out of the house. Well, they both did. You know, the woman and the chap, but the baby wasn't with them. They walked down towards Piccadilly, arm in arm and real cosy like. Upon reaching Piccadilly, they stood chatting for a short time, and then he kissed her hand and walked into the park, the lady though, continued along Piccadilly."

James stood up and rang the bell. Arthur appeared moments later. "Sir?"

"Could you bring some bread and some cold meats please, Arthur. A pot of tea would also be welcome."

"Got any gin or a drop o' brandy?" Pickit smiled, cheekily.

Arthur peered around his employer and looked at Pickit. "Is everything alright, sir?"

"Things couldn't be better, Arthur, thank you. Bring us a couple of glasses of brandy too, please."

When the servant had left the room, James looked at Pickit. "Tell me, what was your impression of the relationship between the couple?"

"I dunno, really. I'm not good at that kind of thing."

"Well, would you have said they were lovers, or just friends?"

Pickit frowned. "I've no idea. When he kissed her, it was on the cheek, but he held her close. You know, like real close. I will tell you one thing though, that baby looked just like him, so it did."

"You were that close?" James asked, surprised.

"Oh yeah, if I had been any closer, I could have heard what they were saying, but they would have spotted me. I was just a little too far away."

Just at that moment, the door opened and Arthur appeared, wheeling a serving trolley.

"Thank you, Arthur, we can serve ourselves," James pulled the trolley nearer the fire. "Oh, do you think you could get a message to Sir William Terrence?"

"Yes, of course, sir." Arthur bowed slightly.

"You do know his address?" James asked.

"Yes, sir, I made a note of it in my day book."

"Good man. Just say that I would like to see him at his earliest convenience, today if possible."

"I will see to it right away, Colonel," Arthur eyed Pickit suspiciously, as he turned to walk away.

Pickit tucked into the meal as if he would never eat another. He also drank the two glasses of brandy. "Are you not having anything then, Colonel?"

James scratched a small spot on top of his head. "Well, I was hoping to share some of that," he frowned, looking at the plates, now almost empty. "Were you hungry by any chance, lad? Stupid question, I suppose."

Pickit's face now turned a deep red. "I thought this was mine, and yours would be here in a minute or two. I'm sorry, you must think I'm a right greedy b...... er, so and so."

James laughed. "Don't worry, it doesn't matter, I'll order some more. I suppose you could eat another helping?"

"And another tot of that excellent brandy, Colonel, if you wouldn't mind. Helps to keep out the cold, so it does." Pickit rubbed his grubby hands together.

"I'm sure it does, though I'm not carrying you all the way to that rat-hole, you call home," James commented, tugging on the bell pull.

Arthur appeared, pushing another trolley of food.

"I presumed that the young gentleman would probably like a little more. I do hope you don't mind, Colonel?"

"Good man." James smiled, and winked at his butler.

"I have sent Lizzie to Sir William's address with a message. I will let you know as soon as she returns," Arthur bowed, and turned to leave the room.

James filled a plate with food before Pickit could demolish the lot.

"Would you make up a hamper for this young man, Arthur? Cold meats, a bottle of wine, a few savouries perhaps?" James asked.

Arthur smiled. "We have a small bottle of brandy. Still good, but not to your usual standard I'm afraid. Perhaps the young sir would like that too?"

"Excellent! Thank you, Arthur. I am sure Master Pickit would make the most of it, and let him sample a small piece of that walnut cake, though not too much mind."

*Chapter 26*

It was mid-afternoon by the time Sir William arrived at James's residence.

Terrence stood surveying the scene. Pickit was asleep in a chair in front of a blazing fire. His boots were warming in the hearth and his bare feet were toasted on the brass fender.

"Good lord, man! Are you opening a home for waifs and strays?" James laughed at the look of shock on his friend's face, and then prodded Pickit's shoulder.

"Wake up, lad. There's someone here who I want you to meet."

Pickit scrambled to his feet and wiped a smear of dribble from his cheek and chin.

"I must have dozed off. Sorry, sir."

"Sir William, meet Mr Pickit. Mr Pickit, this is Sir William Terrence, a friend of mine."

Pickit wiped his hand down his coat, then held it out. Sir William looked horrified, but took of it anyway.

James grabbed a spare chair, and placed it next to his own.

"James, er Colonel Tyler tells me that you might be able to help us." Terrence looked at the boy.

"Actually, he already has," James interjected.

He then went on to tell Terrence all that Pickit had related to him earlier.

"I think we should wait until dark before letting him show us where this man lives. I don't want to be seen, or meet anyone that may know either one of us," James said, now pacing the room.

"I agree. I think though, that I may know the area, if the boy's description is anything to go by. I can't think of anyone I may know who lives around there though," Terrence looked thoughtful.

James looked at Pickit. "You can go home now, but I want you back here at nine tonight. Can you do that?"

Pickit grabbed his boots, and struggled to pull them onto his feet.

"I'll be here. I got a spare set o' clothes. Might be wise if I changed, in case I was spotted."

James nodded. "Well, as long as they are decent and in good repair."

Pickit smiled. "Well, you bought 'em, so you did."

James blushed. "I didn't give you that much money, did I?"

Pickit laughed again. "Let's say, I have a good a tailor, Colonel."

Arthur arrived, and showed Pickit out.

When the two men were alone, they both burst out laughing. When their mirth had subsided, Sir William patted James on the back.

"Well, he may be a rag-tag, but he's a bright rag-tag and actually, very likeable, I'll give him that. I reckon that given the right guidance, we could make something of that young man."

James sat down. "That is my intention, as 'there but for the grace of God...' I was fortunate to inherit a great deal of wealth, and you were born into a privileged family. Things could have been so very different. Either one of us could have been born into his shoes."

"Oh, I agree. It would give me a great deal of pleasure to help someone, something I have never given thought to before," Sir William nodded. "I'm getting quite a warm feeling; I must be softening in my old age."

"Pickit has a friend who has just been shipped off to a penal colony in New Holland. Not only did he provide him with provisions and money for the journey, he's now taken charge of the unfortunate lad's sister, found her a safe place to stay and work. If he can do that, when he has so little himself, just think what we can do for him."

"Why?" William asked. "What is your real reason?"

James shrugged his shoulders. "Thanks to George, I am able to. Without George's generosity, I would be tramping the highways and byways, trying to find the next penny and the next hot meal. I feel privileged, and I am privileged. I want to share some of my good luck with a deserving cause, and that deserving cause, left here a short time ago. I just feel an affinity with the lad, like an older brother if you like."

William nodded. "It's alright James. I totally understand. You are a good man, and I feel privileged to have you as a friend."

"Enough!" James said loudly. "You'll have me in tears in a moment," they both roared with laughter.

Chapter 27

Terrence and Tyler stood side by side on the corner of the street, their profiles hidden somewhat, by the same sycamore tree that had afforded Pickit camouflage earlier in the day. Pickit was pointing through the gloom, to the house that Lady Isobel Banks had visited that morning.

"Are you sure you have the right house lad?" Sir William asked.

"Beggin' ya pardon, sir, I might not be up to your standards, but I ain't stupid. That's the very house."

Terrence blushed and placed a hand on Pickit's shoulder. "Sorry lad, I wasn't in any way questioning your intelligence, it's just that I know who lives there, and not for one moment would I have thought, that the likes of Lady Isobel, would have anything to do with the cad who resides there."

"You know who he is?" James asked, incredulously.

"Oh yes. I most certainly do. His name is Archibald Charles Denton. He has the looks of a Greek God, and the brains of a flea."

James snapped his fingers. "Yes, now I remember. Quite a gambler, or so I have been told. Owes a few people a few pounds here and there."

"Yes, one and the same. Our Mister Denton owes thousands in gambling debts and loans, to an untold number of people, myself included. Quite a cad and a very evasive gentleman."

"So what's he doing with lady Isobel, or more to the point, what is she doing with him?" James asked.

"I bet whatever it is, they ain't up to any good, by what you gents have been sayin'," Pickit butted in.

Tyler and Sir William laughed, softly.

"Definitely not stupid lad, and I do apologise for insinuating that you were," Terrence took hold of Pickit's shoulder and gave it a gentle squeeze.

"S'alright, sir, I ain't offended. It would take a bit more than that."

The three of them ducked behind the tree, as the front door of the house suddenly opened.

James gasped audibly as he watched Lady Isobel kiss the man on the lips. She then walked down the short path. Denton stood on the steps, watching her go. In his arms was a child, who waving vigorously. As she reached the gate, she turned and waved back and blew another kiss.

Pickit grabbed Tyler and Terrence, and the three vaulted over a small garden wall and crouched down, for in a few moments, Lady Isobel would be passing this way, that is, if she were heading for home. James was thankful that it was now quite dark, and they would have to be extremely unlucky for her to have spotted them.

Once her footsteps had receded, and the street was quiet, Pickit chanced a glance over the wall.

"It's all clear, Gents. We can come out now," he said quietly.

"With reactions like that, we could have done with him at Waterloo," James said, pointing to the boy, as they scrambled onto the road.

Terrence was brushing leaves from his coat. "I like him more by the minute."

Pickit could only grin. It made him feel ten feet tall to hear these men actually praising him, something that had been entirely lacking in his life.

"So what are they up to then?" James asked, as they walked back to Park Place.

"Whatever it is, it won't do anyone any good, only themselves of course," Sir William replied.

Pickit, striding along with his hands in his pockets, laughed. "From what you've told me, and what I've gathered, I reckon she's had his kid. She probably loves him, but he ain't got any money, so they can't marry. She knows you had your pal's money, so she's gonna tell everyone that the kid belongs to your pal, so that she gets the money instead of you. They run off and get married, and live in your house and spend all your money, after kicking you out of course."

James and William stopped in their tracks, and looked at the boy, and then at each other.

Pickit who had carried on walking, now stopped and turned to look firstly at James and then at William. "What?" he asked.

"I think you are right," James murmured.

William nodded. "And so do I"

"You do?" Pickit whispered.

The two men nodded simultaneously.

"So what are we going to do then?" Pickit asked, as they walked along the street.

"We?" James asked.

"Well, I thought er...." Pickit stuttered and then became silent.

"If I need you again, I will let you know," James patted the boy's shoulder.

"No doubt we will be in need of your services again, lad, very shortly," William glared at James.

"Er...yes, yes of course," James stuttered. "In the meantime, Sir William and I will get something set up and hope that, given enough rope, she may just hang herself."

Pickit frowned. "She's going to die for this then?"

James laughed, "Good Lord, Pickit, I hope not. It's a figure of speech that is all it is."

Pickit smiled. "Oh! That's alright then. I don't want anyone to die."

"They won't, not by my hand, or anyone else's here for that matter." James assured him, though he wished he could strangle the woman.

*Chapter 28*

James walked down the narrow stairway and into the warm kitchen. Everyone in the room stared at him.

"Sir? Is there something wrong?" Arthur asked and stood.

James smiled. "No, I don't think so. Mrs Ash, what is that delightful smell?"

Mrs Ash blushed. "Tis apples, sir, I'm baking an apple pie," she curtsied lightly.

James rubbed his hands together. "Oh wonderful, that is my favourite."

"Yes, sir, I know," Mrs Ash smiled.

James nodded and grinned at her.

"Is there something I can do for you, sir?" Arthur asked.

"Yes, well I hope so. I would like to arrange a dinner party. Would that be possible?"

Arthur nodded. "Er, yes of course, though, depending on how many guests, we may need to hire more staff."

"It will be a party of approximately five or possibly six people. Please feel free to hire as many people as you think we should need. I would like to put on quite a show. One worthy of a young gentleman of some standing.

"Then we will need a couple of footmen at least, perhaps two or three kitchen maids, and definitely, a second cook," Arthur suggested.

"I will leave all that to you," James nodded.

"May I ask who you will be inviting, Mister James." It was the first time that Arthur had used the informal title to his master. Tyler didn't seem to mind in the least.

"Lord and Lady Banks and Lady Isobel and her guest, and of course, Sir William Terrence and his fiancé who have already accepted, though the official invitations will be going out tomorrow," James thought for a moment. "I am feeling a little devilish, Mr Ash. Do you think I should invite Master Pickit?"

Arthur felt flushed and thought he might have to sit down. "Master Pickit, sir? Do you think that wise?"

James frowned. "Not wise, no. However, I would like him to be here, more as a spectator than anything else."

"As you wish, Colonel."

James smiled and took hold of Arthur's arm. "Don't worry, I am going to place him in your capable hands, for a spot of schooling. You have a week to teach him enough etiquette to get him through the evening."

"A week, sir?" Arthur stepped back in horror. Oh, I think I would need more than a week. A year might be nearer the mark."

James laughed. "Oh, I agree Arthur, but we only have one week. I would not worry too much about his speech; he won't be doing any talking. He will need a little tuition with his eating habits, and of course, manners. On the night, limit the amount of drink he is allowed." Arthur groaned and James laughed.

"Another thing, I want you to take him to a good barber and to a decent tailor. Readymade stuff will be all right for now, but ensure it fits properly. Oh, and make sure he takes a bath, especially on the day before, or even the same as the dinner, if you can. I want that young man looking like he was born with a silver spoon in his mouth."

"May I ask why, sir?"

James smiled and shook his head. "You will find out all in good time, Arthur. Oh, I nearly forgot. He will be staying with us until the night of the dinner. Put him on the top floor, in a room where you can keep an eye on him. I want him to be your shadow from tomorrow onwards. He does nothing without your permission. You have full control."

Arthur felt his heart thudding in his chest. "But what if he er... attacks me or something?"

James grinned. "He won't, believe me."

I think I am about to have a heart attack, sir." Arthur mumbled and grabbed hold of the nearest chair.

James helped the man to sit down. Mrs Ash and Lizzie stood with mouths open, unable to move from shock.

"Look at it this way Arthur," James paced the room with his hands behind his back. "You told me yourself, that had you been younger, you would have been there with the rest of us, thrashing the bones out of Bonaparte. Well, this is your chance to shine, your Battle of Waterloo, if you like." He stopped his pacing in front of his servant and looked down. Speaking quietly he said, "You are not a coward, Mr Ash. You will not turn tail and run like a silly little girl. You will march to the beat of the drum; you will come through this in triumph and I, sir, will not forget the sacrifices made by you and your family. You will be handsomely rewarded for your efforts, Mr Ash." James breathed deeply.

Arthur stood up straight, his face flushed, but now a healthy pink, not the thunderous crimson of a few moments before. "It will be trying sir and no doubt for all of us. Fear not Colonel, we, that is my wife and I and our daughter, will do our utmost to turn that young man into a gentleman," he glanced across at his family, then turned and looked at James. "Now I know why you made the rank of Colonel Sir, a rank richly deserved in my book. I would have followed you into Hell."

James roared with laughter. "Arthur, you are a gem. Nothing less than a diamond. I will now leave Master Pickit in your capable hands. He should be here by eight o'clock this evening. He can try some of your excellent apple pie Mrs Ash," James marched back up the narrow steps, leaving three stunned faces watching his retreating form.

*Chapter 29*

James stood looking through the window, Pickit sat in a chair by the fire, and Sir William Terrence studied a painting that was hanging on the wall between the windows in the drawing room. Georgina, his fiancé, had succumbed to a nasty cold and had been confined to her bed. She had sent her profound apologies to James, promising to meet with him in the very near future. A postscript wished him success in his quest, and William had to admit that he had confided everything to her. She had met and had instantly taken a dislike to the Lady Isobel Banks. Georgina was eager to know everything that happened at the dinner party.

James looked across at the boy. No, he is not a boy any longer, but a handsome young man. He was dressed in a dark blue, high necked, broad lapelled coat. He wore light grey trousers with under shoe straps and shoes of black patent leather. His bright white shirt was tied at the neck with a blue cravat, which was fastened with a ruby encrusted pin. His dark hair was short, falling into soft waves around his ears and neck.

James still couldn't believe the transformation. Arthur had worked hard. Pickit knew how to sit, how to stand and how to walk. He could eat without disgracing himself. He could hold his own in a short conversation, and it was as if someone else had jumped into his body, and taken over.

Pickit could even write his own name, he could read a simple passage from a book, and he could count up to one hundred. These last few parts of his education were due to Lizzie's determination. She had spent endless hours teaching him. Mrs Ash had shown him table etiquette, especially how to sip wine, not guzzle it, and how to carve a joint of meat, or a bird at table. He had learnt the simple manners of life for example "please" and "thank you," and used them often. He would doff his hat to people in the street, whether he knew them or not. He walked tall, with an easy stride, his hands tucked behind his back like a well-bred gentleman.

There had been laughter resonating through the house on a daily basis, and suddenly James realised that Pickit had made the house become alive. It was now a warm and friendly home and James was a proud man.

"We should avail ourselves," James announced looking at his gold pocket watch. "They will be here in at any moment."

Just then, they heard the sound of a carriage pulling up outside. "Everyone to their posts, men," James strode out of the room.

He greeted Lady Sarah and Sir Henry warmly. "It is so good of you to come," he bent over and kissed the back of Lady Sarah's hand, then shook Sir Henry's vigorously.

"It's good to be here, James. It is so lovely to be in this house once more," Lady Banks said.

He greeted Lady Isobel less warmly, but nevertheless with charm.

"I am so glad you could make it. Please let me introduce Sir William Terrence, who I am sure you will have all met."

William kissed the ladies' hands, then shook the hand of Sir Henry. "Good to see you again, William. So, how is that father of yours keeping, well, I hope?" Sir Henry asked. " I do see him at the club occasionally, but he's usually winning the wars all over again."

William laughed. "That certainly sounds like Papa."

James took hold of Pickit's arm. "And this is my ward. Master Pickit is his name, and he is staying here for a while. He is the son of a very good friend of mine, who was lost at Waterloo. I promised I would take care of the boy until he could recover from his loss," Pickit bowed, as he had been taught. Sir Henry looked perplexed. "You seem familiar young man."

"Oh really?" Pickit questioned. "I am afraid I cannot say the same about you, sir, which is unfortunate, as you seem a very nice gentleman. It is a pleasure to meet you," The two shook hands.

Sir Henry laughed. "My mistake, Master Pickit. Believe me, my mistake. You look remarkably like someone I met recently, though actually you are nothing like him."

James inwardly let out a silent breath. Pickit had just passed the ultimate test. They had all known that it would be tricky presenting the lad to Sir Henry. His memory for faces was second to none. Pickit had pulled it off with flying colours.

The dinner was excellent; the conversation articulate and amusing, and the wine flowed generously. Except for Pickit, everyone else's glass was kept full. He feigned an intolerance to too much wine, as it was likely to play havoc with his gut causing him to suffer for days.

"So, my Lady Isobel, I believe my friend James here, extended an invitation for you to bring a guest, and yet you come alone," William said, smiling across at the lady who sat opposite. "You are such a beautiful woman, and yet you are alone."

Lady Isobel blushed. "Oh Sir William, you flatter me so. I am afraid that a few of my friends were rather 'tied up,' and there is no special person in my life at the moment," She took a sip from her wine glass.

"No. I do not believe it," William opened his arms. "I think you are being too modest. I was chatting to that scoundrel Archie Denton the other day, and he indicated that you and he, are walking out together?" Isobel Banks glared at William Terrence, the action not being wasted on him. Suddenly, she smiled.

"I think you are mistaken Sir William, Archie and I are friends, nothing more."

William bowed in apology. "I am terribly sorry my lady, I must have totally misunderstood Master Denton. Too much wine at the time I suppose," he said, never taking his eyes off hers. She quickly looked away.

James leant forward. He hoped he could pull this off as well as Sir William has pulled off his part.

"I feel awful sat here at this table," he hesitated.

"James, are you alright?" Banks asked.

James took a sip of his wine. "Yes, I'm fine, but I do so miss George. He should be here, not me," he didn't miss the greedy gleam in Isobel's eyes.

Banks nodded. "Yes I know the feeling well. He should be here with us. Enjoying a good dinner with his friends. Eventually, it would have been with his own family, someone like you Isobel, possibly children also. However, that is not to be, now." Banks glanced sadly down at the wine glass in his hand.

James couldn't believe his luck. Banks had just given them the opening that they desperately sought.. Before he could speak, William interrupted.

"I do not that think George would ever have married," he announced.

"Why ever not, Sir? George was a very loving boy," Banks said, sternly.

"Ah, that may be so, Sir Henry. However, George had a very serious malady," William argued.

"Go on man, you obviously know something that we don't, though I have no idea why you would be privy to such details, whilst we have been denied any knowledge."

"Oh, I know, only because I was there when something quite catastrophic happened to George," William explained.

"George was badly injured at school in a fight. He was injured so seriously, that he would never have been able to father children. This, of course distressed him immensely, but he was unable to do anything about it. He swore that he would never marry. He said that he could never deny any woman the delight of motherhood," William sighed, then took a gulp of wine.

Sir Henry looked startled, but it was Isobel's face, that really summed it all up. She looked shocked to the core. Her face was pale and devoid of any other emotion. Sir William continued.

"George's mother took him to the best doctors and surgeons that she could find. She spent thousands of pounds trying to find the right treatment, but alas, to no avail. George would remain maimed and celibate for life."

"How on earth do you know all this?" Banks asked, leaning across the table.

Lady Sarah took hold of his arm, "Does it matter Henry?"

Sir Henry patted her hand. "Yes, it does."

William sat back, and related the story that he had told James.

When he had finished, he took another large sip of his wine. "I think George would have been pleased that he died in battle. It would have been the way in which he wanted to go."

James had never taken his eyes off Isobel. She hadn't moved, she hadn't spoken, but her face now held a variety of emotions that no one there could decipher.

James knew he had caught her out. There wasn't any way that she could now blackmail him or drag George's name through the mud. He felt elated.

He sat with one arm across the back of William's chair, and ran a finger on his other hand around the rim of his glass. He was about to speak, but Pickit beat him to it.

"I know Archie Denton." The lad didn't look up from examining a morsel which was left on his plate.

"You do?" James asked, a slight tremor in his voice. He sensed the tension within the room.

Pickit sat back, but his eyes never left the plate. "Oh aye, he does a bit o' gambling at one o' the clubs down on the Strand."

James tapped the boy's foot with his own, under the table. It was the signal for Pickit to watch his words.

"And you know this how...?" James asked, raising his eyebrows.

Pickit now looked up at James and grinned. "Er... sorry, I didn't mention it before, but I was dragged along with a few friends, a couple of times, not that I do much gambling myself. I can't really afford to."

James frowned. "No you can't, and of course, the fact that I don't approve."

Pickit nodded. "Yes sir, but it was only a bit of fun."

"Yes, well. don't make a habit of it," James winked at the lad.

"So, how did you meet the Right Honourable Mr Denton, then?" William asked.

Pickit looked a little uncomfortable, and now wished he hadn't started this.

"He'd been losing quite heavily on this particular evening, and the banker wouldn't extend any more credit. Mr Denton started appealing for a sponsor, but none were forthcoming. He looked a little pathetic sitting there, desperate he was, and so I offered to sponsor him for five pounds."

James looked aghast. "You did what? Are you mad?"

Pickit shrugged his shoulders, keeping up the pretence. "It was only five pounds, sir."

James looked at him. "Only? So, go on then, tell us the rest."

"He did quite well for a few hands, and was actually in credit for a while. Instead of stopping whilst ahead, he continued to gamble, then it was downhill from there on." Pickit looked up at the faces around the table.

"Pah! You should have insisted on his note. You'll never see your money again," William scoffed.

Pickit grinned. "Ah, but I did. He paid me the next day."

William and James both looked surprised. "How did you manage that? I can't get a bean out him," William grumbled.

"It isn't a pleasant sight watching a grown man cry. I had taken a few of my lesser friends with me to see him, they can be a bit scary, especially in the dark," Pickit smiled. "We had to pick him up out of a puddle of his own making."

"I've heard enough gentlemen. Will you please get my cloak?" Isobel had stood, and was now walking around the table.

The two footmen, standing at either end of the room, now scrambled into action as Lord and Lady Banks also stood.

"I'm sorry, James; it seems that we are leaving. Thank you for a wonderful meal, and I hope we can get together soon."

Lord Banks suddenly took hold of James's arm and held him back until the others had left the room.

"Thank you for the insight into that rascal Denton. He's been hanging around Isobel for some time now, and I don't want her getting mixed up with the likes of him. What has been said about him this evening, might have given her more insight into the fellow's character, or lack of it."

The two men shook hands. "Such a shame about George, he seemed to have the whole world at his feet," Banks shook his head as he left the room.

Arthur had managed to procure the carriage, which had arrived in good time. James, William and Pickit stood on the doorstep and watched as it drove down the street and around the corner.

"Did he owe you money?" William asked Pickit as they returned to the dining room.

"Oh yes, though I had forgotten all about it until we started talking about him."

"So, how did you manage that?" James asked.

Pickit grinned. "Let me put it to you this way. How would you like a gang of evil, scruffy, filthy urchins dribbling down your sweaty neck as they dunked you in a cold, filthy, stinking river?"

"Not a pleasant thought, not a pleasant thought at all, dear boy," William said, stuffing another pastry in his mouth.

Chapter 30

A few days later, Pickit and Connie were walking along the Strand. It was early evening and it was busy with hawkers and street vendors. People were going in and out of hostelries and eating houses, a few of the people a little the worse for wear.

Pickit had bought a couple of meat pies from one of the vendors, and now he and Connie were tucking into the hot, tasty food as they sat on a wall. They watched the comings and goings of the busy thoroughfare.

"Would you have liked to have stayed there always?" Connie asked, after Pickit had told her about his stay with the Colonel.

"I suppose so. Plenty to eat and drink, a warm fire and a warm bed. Though I think I would miss the rats."

Connie stared at him. "You'd miss the rats?"

Pickit laughed uncontrollably, for what seemed an age "Not for minute lass."

Connie held his arm and leant in close. "Did he pay you?" she whispered.

Pickit frowned. "He said he had put some money in trust, whatever that means. I can't touch it without his permission though,"

"Well, if you can't touch it, then you can't spend it, I suppose," Connie had kept hold of his arm as they now made their way along Drury Lane.

"How much?" she asked, lightly.

"I dunno. He didn't say. He said that I had done him a huge service and saved him loads of money. If I need any, I have to see the Colonel or, if he isn't available, Sir William. I would have to explain why I wanted it, and then, if it's a good enough reason, I could have it," Pickit explained.

They turned into a short lane and stopped in their tracks. Though it was gloomy here, there was no mistaking the body lying in the middle of the alley, about twenty feet in front of them.

Pickit removed Connie's arm from his, and moved forward slowly.

"It's Jack. It's Mr Scrimms," he said, crouching down, and then turning to look at Connie. Pickit knew there was no mistaking the massive bulk of his employer.

"Is he...is he alright?" she asked, looking over Pickit's shoulder.

"No, I don't know," Pickit could feel the sticky fluid on his fingers.

The man groaned.

"He's alive, thank God!" Connie exclaimed.

The man held Pickit's coat tightly. "Barley," he croaked, and then coughed, dark fluid dribbled down his chin.

Pickit moved closer to the man's face.

"Barley did this?" he asked against Jack's ear.

The man nodded weakly. "Stabbed me, he did, I'll bloody well..." he started to cough again, and Pickit moved away just in time, before blood sprayed his face and clothing.

Jack stiffened, and then lay still, mouth and eyes wide open.

"He's dead," Pickit whispered.

Connie put her hands over her mouth. "What about Mizz Bessie and the babies? Who's going to tell her?" Connie was crying now.

Pickit sat back on his haunches, and then stood up. "Come on. We have to get there before anyone else does," he said, grabbing the girl's hand. They ran on up the alley.

Barley stood in a concealed doorway, watching them. He was trembling violently. The row was, as usual, over money. It had escalated to the point where Jack Scrimms had thumped him in the shoulder. This had incensed Barley and he had pulled the knife. He had stuck it into Jack's ribs before he was even aware that the knife was in his hand. All this had taken place only moments before Pickit and the girl had turned into the alley. He had ducked into the doorway until they had run off along the alley.

He tried to make a move, but then others turned into the alley. He made a run for it in the opposite direction, with the sound of footsteps and shouts, pounding hotly on his heels.

*Chapter 31*

Pickit and Connie had made Bessie sit down and were now plying her with tea generously laced with gin.

"And he definitely said it was Barley?" Bessie sniffed, and wiped her eyes on her apron.

Connie nodded. She was sitting next to Bessie on the wooden settle, and had tried unsuccessfully to put her arm around the woman's massive bulk.

Pickit stood watching them. The room contained an overstuffed couch and other mismatched furniture. It was dark, there was only one lighted candle and the glow from the fire tried desperately to chase away the gloom. A group of children of varying ages sat huddled on the couch in front of the glowing embers.

"I'll be alright, you know," Bessie sniffed. "Jack, with all his faults, was a good husband and father. We never went short. He told me once that this might happen, as he worked in a risky business, but he had provided for us. I have the papers hidden away," she sniffed and gulped the tea.

Pickit looked at her. "It doesn't mean Barley's going to get away with this, Missus," he snarled. "Jack was always good to me too; never saw me short of anything. Barley is going to pay for this."

"Don't you go gettin' yerself into any trouble now, lad. I can't help ya like Jack did."

"Don't worry, I won't," Pickit grabbed his hat and went to open the door. Suddenly it burst inwards, knocking Pickit into the corner behind the door and out of sight. Three Bow Street runners burst into the room.

"Oh, 'avin' a party are we?" the first man asked with a sneer.

"I see that you've heard the news, Missus, that your dearly beloved has departed this world?" the man grinned. "'bout time too, bloody pest he was. Could never get anything over on 'im."

"How dare you speak to her like that, you oaf?" Connie stood and pushed the man backwards. "Have you no feelings?" she pushed him again, harder, and he fell awkwardly against his fellow officers who then all fell down in a heap, one of them banged his head with a thud on the fender. The children sitting on the couch, watched the spectacle and now all joined in, jumping up and down on the men and squealing at the top of their voices. Pickit saw his chance and quietly slipped away.

He ran from the house, wondering which of Barley's 'bolt holes' he would find him crouching in. He had a sudden realisation. Barley wouldn't be hiding; he would be out on the town celebrating, probably.

Pickit checked each and every dive that he could think of. He was careful to who he spoke, and only mentioned Jack or Barley in passing. He didn't want to let on to anyone, that he was actually looking for Jeremiah.

It was by pure chance, that he spotted his quarry in a dirty alleyway, leaning against a doorway, his pants around his knees, obviously relieving himself. Pickit approached quietly. As the man turned, he came face to face with the boy. Pickit was fast, and before Barley could gather his wits, Pickit had hold of his private parts with one hand, and the knife he was holding in the other, was pressed up against Barley's left eye.

"So, Mr Barley, got one over on Jack then, did you?"

Barley whimpered as the pressure on his delicate flesh increased. "I...I never...touched him," he stammered.

"Oh?" Pickit questioned. "Fell on his own knife then, did he? Nothing to do with you then?" Pickit increased the pressure and the man was now standing on his tiptoes.

Barley groaned. "It wasn't meant to happen. It was an accident. He was always pushing me around." he squirmed, trying to relieve Pickit's grip.

Pickit made one quick move, and the knife disappeared from Barley's view. For a moment, Jeremiah wasn't too sure what had happened, but then his gaze dropped to the floor, where he could see his precious member lying in the slime and filth, with blood gushing from a gaping wound between his legs.

With one swift movement, Pickit sliced the man's throat open, quickly stepping back, then running at full pelt down the filthy alley.

*Chapter 32*

James handed him the glass. "Drink it up, it will do you good."

Pickit swallowed the liquid in one gulp, then spent the next minute coughing up his guts, or so it seemed.

Connie stood by him, wringing her hands. "We told him not to go after him," she whimpered.

"Yes, well. I can understand his motives in a way. I believe Mr Scrimms was very good to you both," James answered.

Connie nodded. "He looked after Pickit alright, giving him somewhere to live, and employment when he could. He, or should I say his wife, took me in when I needed a place of safety. They were good people, sir."

"And what of Mrs Scrimms now?" James asked, concerned.

"Well provided for, apparently, Colonel," Pickit said, examining the now empty glass.

The indication wasn't lost on James, and he refilled the glass.

"Can I get you anything, Miss... er?"

"Fowler, Connie Fowler sir. And no, thank you, I don't drink that stuff."

"Tea perhaps then, Miss Fowler?"

She nodded. "Tea would be nice, sir"

Before James could tug the bell pull, there was a light knock on the drawing room door.

"Yes?" James called.

Arthur entered and closed the door quietly behind him.

"Yes Arthur, what is it?"

Arthur frowned. "It's Sir William, sir. He is in a somewhat agitated state. I've shown him to the library."

"What is this? Are we some kind of charitable institution, giving refuge to all and sundry?"

James placed his own glass on a side table. "Will you arrange a cup of tea for Miss Fowler, please, Arthur? Oh and watch him," he pointed to the lad.

He turned to Pickit. "Go steady with the brandy lad. I would like some kept for myself."

James opened the library door, and closed it behind him when he saw the anguish on William's face.

"What on earth...?" James didn't get a chance to finish the sentence.

"She's dead," William said.

"Who is?" James asked. He walked over to a side table and poured two small tumblers of whisky. He couldn't remember drinking so much in such a short space of time. He handed one of the tumblers to his friend.

William downed it in one gulp and James refilled the glass.

"My wine merchant is going to be incredibly rich at this rate," James mumbled.

"It's Isobel and we killed her," William took a swallow of the burning, neat liquid.

James stared at him. "I haven't been out of the house," he defended.

"No, not literally," William waved an arm in dismissal. "She stepped out in front of a brewer's dray, fully laden with barrels."

"Good Lord," James muttered, then sat down heavily. "When."

"About an hour ago. I saw it happen. A right mess, I can tell you." William took another sip.

"How did you come to the conclusion that it's our fault?" James asked.

"The dray was travelling at speed, as they do. She was waiting to cross the road, and she must have seen and heard it coming. She waited; she actually waited, then just stepped out into the road. It was all over in an instant. We had put a stop to her little game, so I believe she couldn't see another way out of her plight."

James stood up. "We are not to blame for this, William. Whatever has happened to that woman, she has brought on herself, do you understand? She would not have hesitated to ruin me if she could, as you well know."

William sighed. "I know you're right, but I feel so responsible."

James nodded. "I do have similar feelings, but my thoughts are now for a little boy who seems to have been an innocent victim in this."

"Ah, that reminds me, James. I was on my way to tell you. That boy is Denton's son and heir, but I can't find the relationship of the child to our lady Isobel, perhaps, there isn't one. I have made endless enquiries, and all I can come up with, is that she was away with friends in the country for most of the spring and summer last year. I believe that she and Denton cooked up a scheme, whereby they would use the boy to get back at you. Lady Isobel would pretend to be his ma-ma and make out that Sir George was the father. Isobel would take care of Archie's debts for the loan of the child. Denton for his part, would swear that he had been asked to take care of the child and keep him from any harm."

"And how did you find this out?" James asked.

"Easy," William smiled for the first time. "I went and spoke to Denton. I mentioned a few things that came up over dinner the other evening. He was more than willing to talk, when I mentioned that Lord Banks might want a few words with him, though he swore, that the Lady Isobel was not the child's mother, he was really adamant about that."

James grinned, "Something has just occurred to me. Over dinner a few weeks ago, someone quoted Shakespeare during the conversation. I believe it was, "The lady doth protest too much, methinks" only this time it was Denton who was protesting."

"You think he was lying?" William asked.

James shrugged. "Perhaps, I don't know. Time will tell, and I now have another problem."

"Oh?" William said.

"Pickit is here. Apparently, there has been a falling out between his bosses. A right couple of thieves. Actually smugglers, or so I've been told. One killed the other, and now Pickit has killed the killer. Slit his throat amongst other things."

William stood up and stared out of the window. "He'll hang if they catch him."

James nodded. "Yes, I know. That's why I'm going to help them move away from London."

"Them?" William looked puzzled.

James smiled. "The boy has a responsibility. A young woman of about his own age. She is the sister of his friend who was transported to New Holland a few weeks ago."

"What are your plans?" Terrence helped himself to another glass of whisky.

"I'm lucky enough to have the means, so I'm sending them both to New Holland. It seems that they really do want to go, mainly because her brother is there. I apparently own a small sheep farm out there, which is supplementing the diet of the penal colony that is nearby, so Pickit can manage the farm for me. There's a small house and a fresh stream on the plot, so they might be all right, if they are prepared to make a go of it. I'll make sure that they are well financed, although Pickit does have some of his own funds to fall back on. Connie will be able to see her brother, and hopefully, they can all make a better life than the one they have here. I was going to send the lad to America, to the plantation there, but then I found out that Miss Fowler's brother was incarcerated in New Holland. I think that would be the best plan, for all concerned. I am not sure what state the farm is in, but the lad says he can handle it, so I'm going to let him. I have told him that if all else fails, he can return here."

"Why are you doing this for him, James? He is nothing to you."

James shrugged. "That's where you are so wrong. The boy saved my life one dark night, and now he has saved all this from Lady Isobel's clutches."

James swept his arm around the room. "With a little help from you, I may add."

William held up his glass in a toast. "Then I shall be at the dockside with you, to see them off," he tipped the glass to his lips.

*Chapter 33*


The next few weeks were very busy for James. The funeral and inquest in the matter of death of Lady Isobel Banks was a traumatic affair for everyone concerned. Suicide was given as the cause, and naturally, Sir Henry and his wife Lady Sarah were devastated at its conclusion.

Sir William Terrence had been mistaken by saying that Lady Isobel was not the mother of the boy in the care of Archie Denton. Denton admitted everything. Isobel had planned to marry him, the father of her child, just as soon as they had the means. However, as it now transpired, they had been tumbled, and she was now dead.

Fortunately, Sir Henry and his wife could not turn away their only grandchild, and vowed to support him and his father as long as Denton agreed to abide by certain rules, as laid down in law by Sir Henry. The child would reside with his grandparents for his own wellbeing, and Denton could have unrestricted access.

James kept Pickit off the streets, by letting him stay out his house. He didn't want him to be questioned by any authority, especially Bow Street.

Connie meanwhile, was helping Bessie get her life into some kind of order. It transpired that the house that she had shared with Jack, now belonged to her, paid for in full no doubt, from funds accrued from her husband's dubious business dealings. Once the warehouse and other holdings with their contents, had been disposed of, she found herself comfortably well off. She wouldn't have to worry about money for a number of years. She had decided to sell the little house just off Duke Street, and being from a farming background, had decided to buy a little place out in the country, and raise a few chickens and small livestock and live off the land. The children would benefit, and if they all pitched in, they would have a good life.

Christmas had come and gone. Any parties or dinners had been small, private affairs.

Sir William and his fiancé, had married in early January, James having had the honour of being best man. The newlyweds had returned to London by the middle of February.

No one was charged with the murders of Jack Scrimms or Jeremiah Barley, though Bow Street were convinced that Barley had killed Jack, after hearing a statement from Bessie, saying that Jack and Barley had always been at loggerheads, especially where business was concerned. Barley always tried to undermine his partner. Bow Street was keen to know who had killed Barley though. Pickit was in their sights, until some nameless snout informed them, that it could have been a moneylender, as Barley was up to his neck in debt.

Chapter 34

Pickit stood at the deck rail, with a bitter wind whipping around his legs. The water was churning and broiling, and the ship swayed and bucked in the choppy seas. Connie huddled close to him with her arm tucked through his. They were wearing thick, warm coats, mufflers and gloves. Down below, in their cabin, stood a trunk containing complete summer wardrobes, ready for their new life.

Pickit and Connie were married the previous morning, before a magistrate, who had been dragged unceremoniously from his bed, and generously bribed into performing the hurried ceremony. They had married because James had wanted everything to be in order and above the law. Pickit and Connie were only too happy to oblige, as it gave them the sense of belonging to someone for the first time in their lives. They were now legally Mr Robbie William and Mrs Constance Fowler. A name change as arranged by James and William as an extra wedding gift, one that Pickit and his bride would cherish.

They both looked down to see their farewell party, which had gathered on the dock. Bessie was in tears and was constantly wiping her eyes on her best lace handkerchief, a brood of children clinging desperately to her voluminous skirts. William and James stood side by side, grinning like a pair of schoolboy idiots. Arthur Ash, his wife and their daughter Lizzie kept waving as if it would make the ship sail away faster. Sir Henry had presented the couple with a handsome set of cabin luggage as a wedding gift, but he was absent from the farewell party due to other pressing engagements.

Pickit looked up at the blue sky, the first England had seen for months. He felt a little sorry for some of the passengers, the ones in the hold that were shackled to each other, another batch bound for a penal colony out in New Holland.

Suddenly the ship lurched, and there was the sound of heavy metal being dragged against ship's sides. The sails were up and billowing out to the full and the ship began to move slowly out with the tide. They would reach New Holland by October hopefully.

Pickit pulled his wife closer, feeling her hot tears against his cheek.

"Sad are you?" he asked, concerned for her.

"On the contrary, I've never been happier in my life," she laughed, and hugged him closer.

15637001R10096

Made in the USA
Charleston, SC
13 November 2012